TRIPLE TROUBLE, VOLUME 1

Trouble Comes in Threes
Storm Warning

Tymber Dalton

MENAGE AMOUR

Siren Publishing, Inc.
www.SirenPublishing.com

A SIREN PUBLISHING BOOK
IMPRINT: Ménage Amour

TRIPLE TROUBLE, VOLUME 1
Trouble Comes in Threes
Storm Warning
Copyright © 2009 by Tymber Dalton

ISBN-10: 1-1-60601-526-5
ISBN-13: 978-1-60601-526-1

First Printing: November 2009

Cover design by Jinger Heaston
All cover art and logo copyright © 2009 by Siren Publishing, Inc.

Printed in the U.S.A.

PUBLISHER
Siren Publishing, Inc.
www.SirenPublishing.com

DEDICATIONS

Trouble Comes in Threes
This one's for Steph, my "psychic twin" who reeeeeaallly wanted a
story about triplet Scottish kilt-wearing shape-shifters.

Storm Warning
To the staff, volunteers, and supporters of animal and wildlife rescue
organizations who fight to save as many as they can every day, not
just when the storms are coming.

Tymber Dalton

Siren Publishing

Ménage Amour

Trouble Comes in Threes

Triple Trouble 1

Tymber Dalton

TROUBLE COMES IN THREES

Triple Trouble 1

TYMBER DALTON
Copyright © 2009

Chapter One

Brodey lifted his nose to the breeze. "Ah, smell that?"

His brother, Cailean, wrinkled his nose. "Smell what?"

Brodey flapped the front of his kilt and grinned. "Freedom!" He playfully rolled the R in a brogue he hadn't really spoken in many, many decades.

Cailean groaned and rolled his brown eyes. "I've never seen a guy who enjoys going kilt-commando as much as you do."

The First Annual Arcadia Highland Games were in full swing.

Apparently, so were Brodey's nether regions.

"Why the hell don't you wear a kilt every day if you love it so much?" Cailean teased.

"Because I don't like getting into fights with redneck assholes at the stockyards and auctions who call it a skirt." Brodey took another swig from his beer. "Where the hell did Ain get to?"

"I dunno. Last time I saw him, he was helping Mark set up the heavy games."

The two youngest of the Lyall triplets studied the crowd. "Doesn't seem the same, does it?" Brodey asked.

"What?"

He shrugged. "Not like the real thing."

"It's Florida in July. What the fuck you think it's supposed to be like, Edinburgh?" Cailean quipped. "I wanted to settle in Oregon when we decided to leave Maine. Noooo, you two assholes decided to move down here."

"Oh, come on, Cail. You're the one who talked Ain into moving to the States in the first place when we left Scotland. I would have been happy going to Australia," Brodey griped.

"Not this *again*. Ninety fucking years of you whining about the same shit. I'm tired of it. You know what they had in Australia back then? Kangaroos, koalas, crocodiles and convicts. You try mating with one of those options, be my guest, asshole."

Brodey was always sullen when he had a couple of drinks in him and hadn't been laid in a few weeks. He finished his beer and tossed the plastic cup into a nearby trash barrel. "Asshole," he grumbled.

Cailean tried to reign in his irritation. "Do us all a favor, Brodey. Go find some chick, get laid, and don't come home until you do." Brodey was the middle boy, middle being relative. Only fifteen minutes separated Cailean and Aindreas, the oldest.

But those fifteen minutes were the difference between Ain being Prime Alpha, and Cailean being the Gamma Alpha. Beta Alpha Brodey's mercurial mood swung between the two extremes, from Cail's laid back, contemplative style, to Ain's sometimes intense kick-ass tude.

Usually, Brodey was more brawn than brain, their resident bonehead. Which was why Cail got stuck doing the bookkeeping for the ranch.

The Lyall boys were identical Alpha triplets except for their eyes. Aindreas had piercing grey eyes, while Brodey's green gaze charmed quite a few ladies. Cail's sweet brown eyes rarely failed to get him a girl—when he could get away from the ranch. They all had jet black hair as of yet untouched by grey.

Not bad, considering they'd celebrated their two-hundred-and-thirty-eighth birthday that past May and didn't look a day over thirty.

Brodey scanned the crowd. "Most of these chicks are either married or jailbait." He snorted. "Or they fell out of an ugly tree and hit every branch on the way down."

Cailean was sick of Brodey's persistent whiny bitching. "I'm going to find Ain," he grumbled. Unlike Brodey, he wore tighty-whities under his kilt, as did Aindreas. He pushed off from the light pole he was leaning against and headed toward the competition area. He heard Brodey behind him.

"Wait for me, jerk."

Cailean didn't slow his pace. It was freaking hot, and he was sick of his brother. Both of them, actually. You didn't hear him grousing. He sucked it up.

He didn't look around as he made his way through the crowd, his mind running in a way he wished his body could. He'd spent more time in the woods lately, stretching his legs and pounding through the brush until he exhausted himself.

That's why he almost missed the faint scent at first. A sweet, fragrant, clean, delicious aroma that made his mouth water and his dick stand up and scream.

He stopped in his tracks. Brodey plowed into him. "What the fuck?" Brodey griped.

Cail held up his hand and closed his eyes, turned in a slow circle, oblivious to the people around them. "Smell that?"

"Aw, fuck me, don't bust my balls—"

"Shut up. Close your eyes."

After a long moment, Brodey's hushed moan. "Holy shit!"

Cail opened his eyes. "You smell her, right?"

Brodey's eyes were still closed. And his kilt looked more than a little tented due to lack of underpinning restraint for his willful cock. "Yeah!" His green eyes popped open. "We've got to find her!"

"We need Ain."

"Fuck that, we need to find *her*!" Brodey frantically looked around. "Where is she? *Who* is she?"

Cail shook his head. "I don't know." He set off, found a stronger whiff. If it was night or no one was around, they could shift and track her. They couldn't very well change into wolves in the middle of thousands of people in a crowded fairground. Might draw some attention to themselves.

They headed off, desperate not to lose her scent, the One they'd searched for since they came of age.

Their perfect mate.

They ran, sniffing, now totally ignoring everyone else, trying to find her.

Her.

Their One.

That both of them instinctively recognized her scent—*her* scent—was proof enough for Cail. Plenty of times one of them had met someone, but the other two didn't react.

They had to find Her.

The men ran.

* * * *

"Laney, wait." Bill shifted the heavy video camera on his shoulder and tried to keep up with her.

Elain Pardie was in no mood for bullshit, especially from her goddamn photographer. "What?" she shot over her shoulder.

"I'm sorry, okay? I thought it was funny."

"It wasn't. And how many freaking times do I have to tell you, do *not* call me Laney?"

He finally caught up with her and grabbed her arm. "You were Laney in school and when we were both carrying cameras. Sorry, *Elain*, but old habits die hard."

She shook free. "I'm trying to make a serious name for myself.

Bullshit like that doesn't help." The bullshit in question being Bill set her up to ask the guys participating in the caber toss what they wore under their kilts.

"It was supposed to be funny."

"I'm sweating my ass off in the middle of Arcadia in freaking July," she growled as she stomped back to the truck. Her shoes were a goddamn mess, the sugar sand from the parking field coating them with grey dust. "That was far from funny."

He had the keys in his hand as they approached the van. She needed to get back to the station and cut the story before the five o'clock news. They didn't have time to cover all the events or even see half the demonstrations, but they had enough footage to work with.

She wouldn't have minded talking to that one guy, the one with the grey eyes, black hair and firm legs, who watched her interview the event organizer.

She'd love to find out what he was wearing under his kilt. That was the kind of guy who should be wearing a kilt, not most of the beer-belly bubbas who had donned them for the day. Too bad he looked so stand-offish.

* * * *

"We'll never find her like this!" Brodey whined. "I've gotta shift."

"How the hell you gonna do that here? Get real." No wonder Ain always made him babysit Brodey. Cail was the cool-headed one. Brodey the bonehead could be counted on to find trouble.

Cail followed Brodey around the back side of a row of wagons selling food. An Italian sausage vendor had a long, canvas skirt snapped around the bottom of his rig. Before Cail could stop him, Brodey dropped to his knees and rolled under. Seconds later, he handed out his clothes.

"Fuck! No, Brodey!"

But it was too late. A huge black wolf with piercing green eyes scrambled out from under the wagon and took off at a full run in the direction of the scent, leaving Cail to juggle Brodey's clothes.

"Fuck!" He ran after him, trying to keep up.

Shifted, Brodey could easily follow the scent. It grew stronger as he raced toward the parking lot. He ignored the people who exclaimed as he brushed past them with his nose to the ground, trying not to lose her.

Mate. Her. Their One.

Desperate, he thought he'd lost her trail as he passed through the front entrance, then realized she'd spent some time there milling around. And he picked up a man's scent with her.

Now tuned in to both, it helped and angered him. A man, with *their* mate.

Brodey was vaguely aware of Cail yelling for him in the distance but he couldn't risk losing her scent.

* * * *

Elain pulled off her sports jacket and hung it in the van while Bill cranked the thing and got the air going.

"Why the hell are they holding this in the middle of summer?" she groused. "It makes no sense."

She slid into the passenger seat but didn't close her door, trying to let some of the heat out. They'd have to drive back to Venice, to the station, so she could get the story edited and filed.

Bill was securing the camera and mic packs in back. "Beats the hell out of me. You'd think they'd want to do it in winter when the snowbirds are down."

* * * *

Aindreas swore under his breath. *Where the hell did those two bozos go?* Something was going on, he'd felt it while that reporter was interviewing Mark, but he couldn't get away to investigate.

There was something about her. He stood upwind from her, but imagined she smelled good from the way she looked. He normally wouldn't mind asking her out. Unfortunately, some lucky guy already had her heart, judging by the rings on her left hand. Reddish auburn hair and blue eyes.

He sighed. One day they'd find Her.

Mark finished talking with the reporter and walked back to Aindreas to chat. Aindreas nervously tried to tune out his instincts, but the more he did, the more he realized he couldn't ignore the feeling anymore.

Once he had a chance to get free he went in search of his two younger brothers. Cail could bust his balls all he wanted about the mere minutes in their ages, but if those two assholes didn't spend their days acting like frat boys, maybe they'd see his point of view. He was Prime Alpha and had a job to do.

Unfortunately, despite traveling all over the world, he hadn't managed to do the most important job.

Find Her.

His father and the other Clan elders had warned that when they came of age the three brothers might never find the One for them, to be their mate. Alpha shifters had to find their One, they couldn't mate for life with just anyone like other shifters could. Twins weren't uncommon, but twin shifter Alpha litters were rare, and they had to find their One together. It proved difficult to get two brothers in agreement on a woman.

Try three. Especially three Alphas.

They were the only known set of living Clan Alpha triplets.

Lucky them. Might as well slap wings on a fucking pig. That thing would probably fly before they located the only One for them.

And at this rate, they might never find Her.

Ain tracked them and…

Aw, hell no. Please tell me he didn't!

Sure enough, when Ain closed his eyes near the Italian sausage trailer, he smelled where Brodey the bonehead had gone from two legs to four.

Fuck!

What the hell would make him shift like that? And why the hell hadn't Cail stopped him?

He picked up his pace, searching for his brothers.

* * * *

Brodey ran, tongue lolling in the heat. Her scent smelled stronger. He was so close. *Please don't let her leave!*

He looked up to avoid a car and that's when he spied the news van, one of five parked off to the side along the fence.

And her scent led right to it.

His heart thumped.

There was a man standing by the open door. In the passenger seat…

His heart nearly stopped as the hot summer breeze carried her scent to him. It was all he could do not to shift right there and pull her from the van and into his arms.

Her. All the bullshit myths about feeling her scent through every cell of his body weren't just bullshit after all. This was way different than any of the false alarms over the years.

The guy was about to close the van's side door and she started to reach for hers. Brodey ran up and barked.

The woman pulled back. "Holy crap, that's a big dog!"

The man backed away.

Whew! The cameraman, they work together. Brodey turned to the woman, then he did something he once swore his pride would never allow him to do.

He sat up on his haunches, whined, and begged.

Chapter Two

Holy crap! That was the biggest freaking dog she'd ever seen in her life!

"Bill, what is he doing?"

Bill nervously shook his head. "Whatever he wants to do. I'm not touching him."

The dog, or maybe wolf hybrid, was jet black with gorgeous green eyes.

Wow, she never knew dogs had green eyes before.

He put his front paws up on her leg, nuzzled her, and whined.

She wasn't much of a dog person, hadn't had one in years since she was a kid. She liked them well enough but didn't have time for one now.

She carefully pushed him down. "Okay, boy. Whatever you are. Sorry, go home or find your family or whatever."

"What is a dog doing loose around here?" Bill asked.

"How the hell should I know, Bill?"

"Want me to get one of the deputies? I think they were doing demos. Maybe he's one of theirs."

"Yeah, good idea. Looks like a K9 dog."

Bill walked off but the dog sat there, staring at her with those intense eyes, still whining. He didn't seem unfriendly.

She got out of the van and knelt by him, feeling through his dense fur for a collar, finding none. "Who do you belong to, boy?"

The woman's intoxicating scent, yet another not-so-bullshit metaphor, sent Brodey's head buzzing.

You. I belong to you.

He rubbed his head against her leg.

A moment later, the cameraman returned with a deputy.

"No, he's not one of ours."

Brodey wrapped himself around her legs, trying to get as much of her scent on him as he could.

"Well, what do we do with him?" she asked.

The deputy shrugged. "I can call Animal Control."

"But they'll take him to the shelter," she protested.

"Well, unless you want to take him. He sure as hell seems to like you. A dog like him, there's got to be someone looking for him." He laughed. "Hey, that's perfect. You can put a lost dog story on the air."

The woman sighed. "I don't want him to get euthanized."

"Then I suggest you take him."

Brodey jumped inside the van. The cameraman looked at her. "I'm not making him get out."

She rolled her eyes. "Fine. Let's get going. We're going to be late."

They shut the doors and pulled away.

It was only after Brodey forced his way between the front seats to lay his head on her lap, his eyes closed, inhaling her scent, that he realized what he'd done.

Aw, fuck. Ain and Cail are gonna kill me.

* * * *

Cail scanned the parking field. He'd totally lost the scent. Not just the woman, but now Brodey, too.

Fuck!

They were parked near the fence in exhibitor parking. He dropped Brodey's clothes into the back of their truck and then ran to where he lost the scent. Aindreas walked up a few minutes later.

"Where have you two been?"

"No time for that now. I can't find Brodey."

Aindreas dropped his voice. "Why the fuck did he shift?" he growled.

"No time for that!"

"Yes, time *right now*." He fixed Cail with his grey eyes. Cail had to defer to the Prime.

"We were following a scent. It's Her, we smelled Her! The One!"

Ain groaned. "Fuck me. You two assholes are killing me. Ever hear the story of the wolf who cried mate one too many times?"

"Smell for yourself!"

Ain shook his head but closed his eyes. All he could smell now were cars. There was a hint of something, very faint, but in the dry dust and with all the cars and people who'd been through there, and livestock in the cattle complex next door, he wasn't anywhere close to declaring Her found. "All I smell right now is the ass whooping I'm itching to dish out to you two. Where the hell is Brodey?"

"I don't know! He shifted to try to find her. I'm telling you, we both smelled her!"

A car honked at them and they stepped out of the way. They spotted a deputy nearby, directing traffic into the parking lot. Ain took a chance.

"You didn't happen to see a huge black dog around here, did you?" Ain asked. "He...uh...slipped his leash while we were trying to get him out of the crate. He's supposed to be part of the herding demonstration."

"Oh! That was your dog?"

Ain felt his gut roll. "Was?"

The deputy smiled. "He's okay. He jumped into that news crew's van and they took him. She didn't want to send him with Animal Control."

Inside their truck, Cail quietly sat in the passenger seat while Aindreas screamed and pounded his fists against the steering wheel in anger. When he finally got himself under control, he glared at his brother.

"Now we have to figure out which fucking station it was since Deputy Dipwad didn't notice."

"Well, how many could there be?"

"They were all here at some point in time today, asshole. From Tampa down to Naples, and even crews from Orlando and Miami. Mark said there were at least twenty different TV crew passes issued for stations from around the state."

Cail cringed. "I'm sure he'll call."

"A fucking NEWS CREW! Could he try any harder to put us on the fucking radar? One thing. One *goddamned* thing. I wanted to spend a day helping out an old buddy, have some fun, relax and chill, and you two fucking assholes can't stay out of trouble when my back is turned?"

"It was Her," Cail insisted. "I swear to the Goddess, man, it was Her. We both smelled her."

Ain started the truck and backed out. "You better hope so. Because if she's not, I'm going to neuter both of you and it won't be an issue anymore."

* * * *

Brodey was in heaven. Goddess help him, he didn't want to move from his spot. He'd learned Her name was Elain. He read it when she hung her press pass on the rearview mirror.

Beautiful!

She hesitantly rested her hand on his head and scratched him behind the ears.

"He's big," she said to the man, whose name he'd learned was Bill.

"Probably a wolf hybrid. They get big."

"You want to take him?"

"Are you shitting me? My wife would kill me. Our cat hates dogs.

You volunteered, you're stuck with him."

"He seems clean, no fleas, he's not even dirty." She scratched him behind the ears again.

Brodey knew if he was a cat he'd be purring.

Somewhere in the depths of his brain it registered that he'd fucked up royally, and that when he finally got back together with Ain and Cail, they were going to kill him.

But he'd found Her.

He knew it.

* * * *

Ain drove them home to their cattle ranch fifteen minutes from the fairgrounds. Three thousand acres, lots of woods, and a perfect place to lay low.

"I'm gonna kill him," Ain muttered.

Cail grabbed Brodey's clothes from the back of the truck and followed his brother inside. "What do we do?"

Ain glowered at Cail. "You are gonna sit your ass down and stay the hell out of trouble while I try to figure out where Bonehead went." He booted up his laptop and did a search for Florida TV stations, printed a list, and started calling. Being a Saturday, most of them were staffed by skeleton crew who gave him the same old, "Yeah, if we hear anything, we'll let you know," line. If they even answered at all.

After an hour, Ain gave up and went to the kitchen to fix himself something to eat.

* * * *

Brodey followed Elain from the van into the TV station, never allowing himself to get more than a few steps away from her. No one would separate him from her again. Ever.

He was oblivious to all others. When she sat, he immediately curled at her feet, part of him always touching her.

Her.

His Mate.

Mine.

After she finished her work, she looked down at him. "I suppose you're going home with me, dude. We'll have to stop and get you something to eat."

He followed her out to her car and immediately jumped into the backseat when she opened the door. As she drove, he closed his eyes and rested his muzzle on her shoulder over the back of the seat.

When she stopped at a shopping plaza he worried he might have to stay in the car, but she let him get out with her.

"I guess I don't have to worry about you running off the way you're glued to me," she said with a laugh.

Their destination—a pet store. Inside she bought him a collar and leash, bowls, and a huge bag of top-dollar homeopathic dry dog food. When she put the collar around his neck he pressed his head against her.

Please. Keep me. Mine.

She could lead him by a leash or by his dick, he didn't freaking care. As long as he was with her.

Her.

The kibble wasn't too bad, sort of like beef-flavored dry cereal. He'd eaten worse. When she went to bed, he carefully crawled up onto the mattress next to her and breathed a sigh of relief when she didn't make him get down.

Elain spent a restless night dreaming about a hunky, kilt-clad guy with black hair. She recognized him as the guy she'd seen at the Highland Games—figures—but he had the dog's green eyes in her dream, not the piercing grey eyes he'd had in real life.

Far be it for her to fight a damn good wet dream. Especially considering it was the only kind of two-person sex she'd had in over a year. She rolled over in bed and plunged her hand between her legs, squirming against the sheet as her dream lover showed her how much he packed beneath his kilt.

A lot.

In her dream, he sank his thick cock inside her, fucking her hard and fast in a way no man had ever fucked her. As her dream lover fucked her, her fingers stroked her clit, drawing her close to release.

Brodey softly whined. He was vaguely aware of a puddle of drool forming under his muzzle as he watched her finger herself. It was all he could do not to shift back and help her. He knew he couldn't help her like this.

Not that he didn't want to—fucking Ain and his Prime edicts. Don't reveal yourself to Outsiders. No lupine loving unless we're mated.

Fuck. Once Prime laid down the law, he had to obey it.

She smelled soooo good. The sweet, musky aroma of her dream passion practically bowled him over. There was no way she couldn't be their One.

He drooled.

The next morning, Elain awoke hours before dawn, then took a shower after walking Brodey. Apparently she had to be at work early. "You're going with me," she said to him. "Lucky you, the boss likes dogs. Maybe he'll take you."

Brodey whined.

He realized he fucked up, but he couldn't lose her. There was no way to call Ain and Cail, they had to be going batshit by now.

The night spent with her only cemented his conviction. She was, without a doubt, their mate. Never before had he felt like this, ever.

He rode with her to the station and followed her around all morning. When it came time for the morning news, he realized too late he was a star of a segment. He'd been too busy inhaling her scent and listening to her lyrical voice to pay attention to her actual words.

"…so if you know who he belongs to, or if you can prove you're the owner, please contact me here at KVPN at 555-6822, extension 206."

Aw, fuck.

At lunch, she snuck him a few pieces of bread from her sandwich. He gently took them from her hand, making sure not to nip or slobber on her.

Elain patted his head. "I sort of hope no one claims you."

As stupid as it was, and as much as she didn't want or need a dog, he was sort of nice to have around. He wasn't anything like any other dog she'd ever had. Definitely smart and well-trained. Someone had to know who he belonged to.

When she was ready to leave at three, no one had called. She admittedly felt a little relieved about that.

"Let's go, boy."

Brodey followed her outside to her car. It was only as they were driving home that he finally noticed her rings.

What the fuck?

That was a wedding band, no mistake, on her left hand. And an engagement ring.

His heart curled. *No, please, Goddess, no!*

She couldn't be married, she couldn't belong to someone else, not when she was perfect for them!

He tried to think rationally. There was no scent of a man at her house, not even a hint of one. Widowed?

As sick as it sounded, he could only hope, because otherwise that might mean long-distance relationship.

And that would mean she was off-limits.

Brodey whined.

Chapter Three

Cail avoided Ain most of the day, spending much of his time surfing the Internet websites for the various TV stations and online found pet ads. By seven, Ain was nastier than ever and Cail didn't even attempt to speak to him.

At seven-thirty, Cail found it and breathed a sigh of relief. On the KVPN website, a video clip, Brodey staring up at…

Her.

He couldn't smell her but the obvious look on Brodey's face told him that was her.

And she was…

Fuck. A TV reporter.

Cail groaned and leaned back in his chair. *Son of a bitch.*

"What?" Ain called from the kitchen.

"You'd better come see this." He played the clip for Ain, who closed his eyes and groaned.

"That stupid fucking asshole." It was the reporter who'd interviewed Mark at the Highland Games. The married one.

"That's Her."

"She's a goddamn reporter! I don't give a shit if you two dicks want a piece of ass—"

Cail stood, angry. "That's *Her*! We both smelled her, I'm telling you!"

Ain glared. "*No more.* Stop. *Now.* How many other times over the years have one of you claimed you found Her? I'm sick of this shit! Besides, didn't you see her hand?" He pointed at the screen. "She's married, asshole."

Cail's heart fell. No matter what, they were bound by the Code of the Ancients. That meant you didn't take another's mate, even if she was the One for you.

"No," he whispered, collapsing into his chair, devastated.

"Yeah. So suck it up." Ain played the video one more time and wrote down the number. "I'll call her and ask her where I can meet her to pick up our 'dog.'" He stormed out of the study.

Cail stared at the frozen image on the screen. Ain didn't understand because he hadn't smelled her. He was vaguely aware of Ain calling, speaking, then hanging up.

"Voice mail," Ain said from the living room. "If the phone rings, *I* answer it."

Cail didn't respond, still staring at the screen.

* * * *

Brodey moped. Elain patted the couch for him to jump up next to her. He did but he couldn't take his eyes off her rings. There were scattered pictures of her around the house with others, as a child and adult, but nothing he'd label a wedding picture. He couldn't very well snoop through her desk until she was asleep.

In her closet, only women's clothes. No hint of a man except in an old, leather jacket he suspected was nearly as old if not older than her.

His heart ached, his body ached to hold her, his dick ached to plunge inside her and claim her. Not that he could until after Ain took her for them, but still...

Brodey whined.

Before she went to bed she dialed into her office voice mail. He watched as her face fell. She looked at him. "Your name's Beta?"

Brodey whined again and laid his head on his paws. *Dammit, Ain and Cail must have seen the video.*

She jotted something down and then hung up. She looked nearly as upset as he felt.

Elain knelt next to him. "Hi, Beta."

Brodey raised his head. That Ain had used birth order instead of his name spoke to how truly pissed he was. There would be no hope of staying with Elain, even shifted, once she took him back to Ain. Prime declared, and Beta followed. That was the way.

He licked her face, enjoying the sweetly salty taste of her flesh. Truly perfect.

"I guess I'm taking you back to your daddy tomorrow."

Well, close enough, babe.

"I've got the day off, so I'll drive you home. I'll wait until tomorrow morning to call though."

Brodey consoled himself that he'd get to sleep with her one more night.

* * * *

The next morning, Ain grabbed the phone on the second ring. "Aindreas Lyall."

"Mr. Lyall? My name is Elain Pardie. You called about the dog."

Ain breathed a sigh of relief. He'd spent a restless night waiting for her call, and it was now eight in the morning. "Yes, thank you. I'm so glad you found Beta. We've been very worried about him."

"How did he get loose?"

"We were doing a herding demonstration and somehow he slipped out of his crate when we weren't looking. A deputy told us he left with a news crew but we weren't sure which one."

"Well, I have the day off. I don't mind driving him home. If you'll give me your address, I'll get a bite to eat and bring him back for you."

Cail stood close and listened. It was Her! Even through the phone her voice carved a chunk out of his soul. How could Ain *not* feel it? Once he smelled Her, he had to agree she was their One.

His brother gave her directions and then hung up and glared at Cail. "You *will* shift when she gets here."

"Why?"

"Because we don't have papers on our 'dog,'" Ain growled. "If she sees you, his twin, she'll turn him over without question."

Cail had no choice.

Fucking Prime edicts anyway.

A little after eleven, Ain stuck his head in the front door. Cail had been working on bookkeeping for the ranch. "Go shift and get your ass out here. She's coming."

"Bastard," he muttered. But he stood, stripping his shirt as he walked to their shared bedroom. He left his clothes on the bed and shifted, then trotted out the front door. Ain had left it standing open for him.

When she pulled into the driveway, Cail fought the urge to race to meet her and jump into the car when she opened the door. He spotted Brodey in the backseat. When she opened her car door he nearly fell over from the sweet scent.

Her.

There was no doubt.

From the slightly glazed look in Brodey's eyes, he knew he was right.

Ain walked from around the side of the house but didn't get too close. "Hi, Ms. Pardie?"

"Elain's fine." She opened the back door but Brodey was in no hurry to get out.

Cail didn't blame him.

Ain saw his hesitation. "Beta, *come*."

Prime voice. Brodey dipped his head and slowly jumped out. He paused next to Elain, nuzzled her hand before he slowly walked to Ain and lay down in front of him.

Cail dashed up to her and nosed her hand before Ain could order him back.

He closed his eyes and deeply inhaled. *Her…*

"Gamma, *come*."

Fuck.

With his tail between his legs, Cailean turned and walked over to Ain, lying down next to Brodey. He couldn't resist leaning over and sniffing his brother's coat. He smelled like Her.

Elain shut the car doors and walked over, stopping behind them. "Wow, they look identical. How do you tell them apart?" He was *the* guy! The same hunky kilt dude from the Games. *And* her dreams. *Yowza!*

His grey eyes tore something right through her. Today he wore snug jeans that she'd love to help him out of, and a button-up work shirt that covered far too much of his firm torso.

"Their eyes. Beta's eyes are green. Gamma's are brown. And their personalities. Beta's a whiner." He looked down at his dogs. "Their other brother, Alpha, has grey eyes. He's around here somewhere."

The deep, resonating tone of Lyall's voice stirred something inside her. "Well, I'm sorry you were so worried. We would have hung around a little longer, but I was on deadline. I didn't want to send him to the shelter."

"It's okay, Ms. Pardie. We appreciate you taking care of him."

"Elain, please."

"Elain. My brothers will want to thank you personally. They'll be out in a moment." He looked down at his dogs. "House. *Now*."

The two dogs immediately stood and trotted toward the house.

"They're very well-behaved."

"Normally. Yesterday was unusual. I hope he didn't cause you any trouble. I'll be happy to reimburse you for anything you spent on him, and for your time and gas to drive out here."

"No, that's okay." Elain stepped a little closer, but was it her imagination he stepped away?

Ain had to step back. *Aw, fuck! The assholes were right!*

As she stepped closer, he took another step back. He had to, or he would grab her and kiss her. He tried to focus on her wedding rings. *Taken. She was taken.*

He wanted to cry but he'd never let his brothers see. No matter how his heart was breaking.

Cail and Brodey appeared a moment later and stood behind Ain. He sensed their tension, their eagerness to be with her.

He had to get her out of there. *Now.*

Elain stared. *Holy crap, times three!* They were identical hunks, wearing different shirts, the other two brothers barefoot but in jeans and work shirts.

No, wait, not quite identical. One had green eyes, one had brown, while Aindreas had grey eyes. And the green-eyed cutie's hair was the same thick, black mop but slightly longer than his brothers' neatly trimmed hair.

"My brothers, Cailean," Aindreas nodded toward the brown-eyed babe, "and Brodey," he indicated the green-eyed gorgeous guy.

"Pleased to meet you," she replied, hoping she didn't drool. What the hell was *wrong* with her?

The two brothers smiled and nodded but made no move to step forward. They stood behind Aindreas. She got the impression he was in charge even though they were obviously triplets.

Weird.

"Again, thank you so much for driving all the way out here," Aindreas said. "We greatly appreciate it."

"No problem." She licked her lips, struggling for a reason, any excuse, not to leave. "Um, do you train dogs professionally?"

He crossed his arms. "We're a working ranch. Some skills are necessary."

Aindreas tried not to breathe through his nose, which made his problem worse. The breeze was blowing from behind her, putting him downwind and bringing her scent right to him. He could taste her on the wind as he inhaled through his mouth.

"I'd love to see a demonstration sometime."

He curtly nodded. "I'd be happy to, but I'm afraid today we've got a lot of work to do. Perhaps another time. Thank you for taking the time to bring him back, and have a safe drive home."

Well, okay then. Grey Eyes turned and started toward the house, leaving the other two brothers standing there staring at her like they wanted to talk.

She was about to say something when Aindreas turned. "Brodey, Cailean, we have a lot of work to do. *Now.*"

The way he emphasized the last word, she almost felt compelled to follow them, and nearly took a step forward toward him.

The two men bashfully smiled, turned, and followed him into the house.

She swallowed hard, feeling a little…empty. How freaking stupid was that? Elain realized a moment later she was still standing, alone, in the Lyall's yard. She reluctantly got in her car and left.

For the next two days, every time she had a moment to herself she thought about the brothers. And how much she missed Beta. She took what was left of the dog food and dropped it off at the Humane Society shelter, along with the bowls and leash and collar.

Stupid. She never should have got her hopes up.

She kept trying to come up with excuses to call Aindreas Lyall, wanting to set up an appointment to get a demonstration, and knew she couldn't. Not from his chilly response.

He's probably married. Or gay. Or sociopathic.

But as cute as he was, not to mention his two brothers, a gay, married, sociopath might not be a bad thing to have in her life.

Would be worth it to not be alone anymore.

She twisted her grandmother's rings on her finger. They'd been helpful keeping the creeps away. It was only after she'd talked with Lyall that she realized she still had them on. *Damn.* The one time she really wanted a guy to ask her out and she probably queered it.

Terrific.

* * * *

Brodey and Cail no sooner had the door shut behind them that they were after Aindreas, begging. "Please," Brodey said, "you can't tell me you didn't smell Her!"

Aindreas glared. "Drop it. *Now*. She's married, asshole."

"No! I don't think so! There was no man—"

"NO MORE!" Andreas roared. "Do *not* talk to me about her being the One again. Period. *End of subject*." He stormed out the back door, slamming it behind him.

Brodey wanted to cry. Fucking Prime edict.

He dragged Cail into the bedroom and closed the door. "It's Her!"

"What about her husband?"

"There was no man there, anywhere, not even the scent of one! The only men she had contact with while I was with her were her coworkers. She didn't even talk to any guys on the phone unless it was work related."

"What about her rings?"

Brodey shook his head. "I don't know. I didn't have a chance to do any snooping. All I know is there hasn't been another man in her house in I don't know how long. No men's clothing in the closet. Nothing."

Cail chewed on his lip. Brodey knew if someone could find a loophole around the edict, Cail would.

"We need to go talk to her."

Brodey sighed. "Ain said we couldn't."

Cail grinned. "No, he said we couldn't talk to *him*."

Brodey's grin matched his brother's. "Genius!"

Chapter Four

Cail and Brodey waited a couple of days to let Ain settle down. He acted surly and bad-tempered. Cail suspected Ain had sensed Elain Pardie was their One.

But as Prime, once Ain had seen her rings he'd shut down, knowing he had to enforce the Code regardless of how irrational his refusal to talk with them was. With Brodey and Cail now forbidden to talk to Ain about it they had to be sneaky.

Brodey and Cail waited until they needed a trip into town for groceries. They grabbed quick showers, changed clothes and jumped in the truck before Ain could figure out their plot. They headed straight for Venice.

Brodey directed Cail to the TV station. The sight of Elain's car parked outside brought a grin to both men's faces.

"Yes!" Brodey cheered.

They walked in and stopped at reception. It was a little after two, maybe they could talk Elain into a late lunch with them.

Brodey smiled at the receptionist. "We're here to see Elain Pardie. Brodey and Cailean Lyall."

The receptionist smiled and nodded. "I'll call her." Normally, Brodey would try to get into the woman's pants, she was a cutie.

But not now. Not since they'd found their One.

A few minutes later, Elain walked out and both men resisted the urge to step forward and hug her. Brodey had agreed to let Cail handle the talking.

"We wanted to know if we could take you out to eat. I'm sorry we were busy the other day, lots of things going on. We realized we might have come off as a little rude."

Elain's heart raced. These two hadn't come off rude, but Aindreas sure as shit had. Even though she'd had a sandwich a few hours ago and wasn't really hungry, she nodded. "I'd love to. I need to finish a couple of things, then I'll be ready."

"We'll wait out here for you."

"Okay!" She looked from Cailean's brown eyes into Brodey's green gaze. Something about his eyes looked oddly familiar. Deep inside her, something contracted in a hot and pleasant way. This was trouble. Double trouble. Twin hotties.

Make that triple trouble.

Except as cold and distant as the other brother acted, maybe that wasn't an issue.

She raced through a few calls, her hands trembling. *Stupid. They've got to be taken. And how could you pick one over the other?*

She shivered as a deliciously naughty thought crept to mind. She stamped it into submission. No, *hell* no. That was just...

Having the two brothers would be a h-h-hottttt fantasy, but never something that would happen in real life.

They were still waiting when she returned. "Where to?" she asked.

Cailean smiled. "Wherever you'd like to go. Our treat."

How about back to my house and to bed?

Argh!

She licked her lips. "There's an Applebee's down the road."

The brothers nodded.

They followed her. She wanted to accept their invitation to ride with them in their truck, but somehow she didn't trust herself.

The restaurant lot was full. She had to park behind the building in an adjacent parking lot. At least it was shady there. The brothers parked next to her, between her car and the restaurant. Nervously trying to make small talk, she walked between them to the restaurant.

While they waited to be seated she fought the urge to take and hold their hands.

What the *hell* was wrong with her?

They didn't take their eyes off her and that was no exaggeration. And not in a creepy, Internet stalker kind of way either. A passionate intensity that totally drenched her panties.

She hoped she didn't leave a damp spot on her skirt.

She could barely think straight around these two men. They had a three-hour meal, mostly talking instead of eating, and she learned they were cattle ranchers on the family spread in Arcadia, last of an increasingly rare breed in Florida.

"So where's your other brother?" she finally asked.

Cail, as he'd asked her to call him, shrugged. "Ain's busy. Lots of work to do." He winked. "We escaped. We're playing hooky. We wanted to see you."

She couldn't stand it anymore. "Your wives won't mind you having a long lunch with a strange woman?"

They grinned. "We're not married," Brodey said.

God, his green eyes were gorgeous!

"No girlfriends, either," he added. "Single and available."

She thought she might have moaned. *Fuuuck me!*

"What about you?" Cail asked, nodding toward her left hand. "How long have you been married?"

She blushed. "No, I'm not married. Not even dating."

Did both men suddenly freeze? Cail spoke again. "What about your rings?" he asked in a careful, cautious tone.

"I just wear them to keep from getting hit on. They belonged to my grandmother."

The men looked at each other and broadly grinned.

"What?" she asked.

Brodey laughed and seemed to relax. "Nothing. We just thought you were married."

"Oh, no. Never been married. Haven't had a relationship or even a date in over a year."

She couldn't put off the inevitable. "Well, thank you both, this was wonderful. I have an early day tomorrow and need to get home so I can get to bed. Three a.m. wake-ups come way too early." She'd love to crawl between the sheets with either or both men.

Her heart fluttered at the thought. Well, maybe not heart. The sensation was centered lower, between her legs.

The men paid the bill and walked her out to her car. Cail walked between the vehicles ahead of her, then turned to face her.

"You're beautiful, Elain," he whispered.

She gasped at the emotion in his voice. How could he have this effect on her? "Thank you."

She was aware of Brodey stepping close behind her. The heat from his body washed through her even though they weren't touching.

"Very beautiful," he whispered in her ear.

She closed her eyes, fully aware that she was rapidly approaching an uncharacteristic loss of control with these two guys.

When Cail kissed her, his gentle, feather-light touch made her moan. She grabbed his head and buried her fingers in his hair, crushed her lips against his.

Brodey definitely moaned behind her and pressed his body into hers. She felt his hard erection through his jeans, and as he forced her against Cail, she felt his as well.

Cail dropped to his knees. She was vaguely aware that even though they were mostly shielded by the two vehicles, they were still in public.

Brodey's hands cupped her breasts through her shirt as he pulled her against him. "Close your eyes and relax," he whispered against the side of her neck. "No one's around."

She threw her head back against his shoulder, glad to take his advice, instinctively sensing these two men wouldn't let anything bad happen to her.

Cail ducked under her skirt. She didn't protest when he tore through the crotch of her panties, then pushed her legs a little further apart. His tongue, scorching hot, circled her clit before dipping deep inside her.

She moaned. This had to be another hot dream. Shit like this just did *not* happen in real life!

Brodey kissed her, his tongue and hers dueling as Cail quickly brought her to the most explosive orgasm she'd ever had in her life.

Weak and unable to move, she let Brodey hold her. Cail stood, then unlocked their truck's passenger door.

"My turn," Brodey said as he effortlessly lifted her to the seat and pushed her onto her back. Before Elain could protest, he'd thrown her skirt up and buried his face between her thighs, her legs draped over his shoulders.

Elain closed her eyes and moaned. Cail's fingers laced through hers. "Give it to him, baby," he encouraged. "Jesus, you're perfect."

Brodey's tongue probed her, fucking her, then laving her clit before plunging deep inside her again.

If they were this good with their mouths…

Holy fuck!

She exploded, crying out as her climax hit. Then she lay on the seat and gasped for breath.

As reality crept back in she realized what she'd just done. She'd let two guys, strangers, make love to her. In public.

Embarrassed, she sat up and pushed her skirt down. But the men looked…

She'd never had a guy look at her like that before.

Like they were in love.

"Are you okay?" Cail asked.

She nodded. Brodey helped her out of the truck, then he pulled her into his arms again and kissed her. She wanted to—

No!

"I need to get home," she mumbled, fumbling for her purse and keys, which she'd dropped.

Cail stroked her cheek and leaned in, nuzzling her, inhaling deeply like he was smelling her. "Can we come with you? Please?" he softly asked.

She shook her head. "No! No, I'm...I'm so sorry. I don't know what got into me..." She reddened, her hands shaking as she tried to unlock her door. She couldn't be alone with them! She didn't know what the fuck was wrong with her, but if she was alone with them she would be well and truly fucked.

Literally.

Wait, why is that a problem?

"I'm...thank you for lunch." She avoided their eyes and reluctantly pulled out of Brodey's grasp. At first she wasn't sure if he'd let go of her, but he reluctantly did after placing a tender kiss on the back of her hand.

She locked her doors and took a deep breath before starting her car and backing out of the spot. She had to pull over on the way home to calm herself. And she cried.

Once home she took a shower, crying even harder. She didn't know if it was because of what she'd done, or what she didn't do— refusing their request to come home with her.

One thing was for certain, she felt even hornier now than before, the memory of what they'd done to her bouncing around in her brain.

She grabbed her shower massager and used it to have three more orgasms that weren't nearly a fraction as satisfying as the two the men had given her in the parking lot.

And she was still horny.

Elain wasn't sure she'd ever fall asleep. Finally, two hours before her alarm went off to wake her for work, she did.

* * * *

Cail and Brodey watched her drive off. In silence they climbed into the truck and Cail started it. They sat there with the air running and their eyes closed, inhaling the traces of her scent that still lingered in the cabin.

"You felt it, right?" Brodey whispered.

"Yeah," Cail said, his hoarse voice full of emotion. "I don't give a shit what Ain says. She's our One."

"Goddess, I wanted to fuck her."

"We can't."

"I know."

Cail opened his eyes. "We can't even get a goddamned blow job from her," he grumbled. "Not until we figure out how to get Mr. Prime Asshole to listen to us and get off his fucking high horse." He angrily shifted the truck into reverse and backed out of the space.

Code of the Ancients—Prime first when finally taking their One mate. Normally that applied to twins but since they were triplets it still had the same effect. Ain had to be the first to take her like that. Any of them could sleep with other women until they were mated, but with their One it had to be Prime first.

And now, of course, that they'd found their One, they couldn't sleep with anyone else anyway. Not that they'd want to even if they could. No other woman could ever compare.

They barely remembered to buy groceries before they returned home. Aindreas was too mad to scream. When he got close enough to them to smell them he froze.

"What the hell did you two do?" he growled.

Cail and Brodey exchanged a nervous glance. Cail scrambled for an approach Ain wouldn't clamp down on and that wouldn't be squelched by the Prime edict. "Some women wear wedding rings when they're not married. As a way to keep men from hitting on them."

"Do *not* tell me you went and saw her."

The brothers kept their mouths shut.

Ain turned, pacing, running a hand through his hair. Between his rage and the totally fucking distracting smell of Her on them, he couldn't think. He wanted to grab them and slap the shit out of them and then smell them where they still bore her scent.

"I told you to drop this. How could you defy me?"

"You told us not to talk to you," Cail shot back. "If you'd quit being an asshole, let us talk to you, we can solve this whole thing in five damn seconds."

Aindreas stormed out the back door, slamming it behind him. He looked only marginally calmer when he returned a few minutes later. "Okay, fine," he spat. "Get it out and over with."

Brodey and Cail exchanged another glance. Cail spoke. "They're her grandmother's rings. She's not married, not seeing anyone. She only wears them to keep from getting hit on." He glanced at Brodey again. "She's not taken."

"What did you two do to her today? You know damn well we're not forcing a woman to be with us."

"Believe you fucking me, there was no force involved." Cail related the events in the parking lot.

Ain moaned. "You stupid assholes. How could you do that to her?"

"What? We didn't take her, we didn't mark her!" Not that they could without Ain anyway.

Ain shook his head. "She needs to be able to make her mind up about this. If she really is our One..." He groaned, sat, hung his head. "No, you didn't mark her, but it's going to be agony for her now."

Brodey knew he wasn't always quick on the uptake but this really confused him. "What the hell are you talking about?"

"She has to submit, dumb fuck. Willingly. I already told you guys years ago that when—*if*—we found our One, I would *not* force her. I wanted someone who willingly wanted to be with us. You haven't told her anything about shifting, mating, marking, the ceremony, any of that. If she decides she can't handle it, she's not going to be able to walk away and never look back. Not after what you two losers did to her. *And* she's a fucking reporter!"

Cail's heart fell. "Oh." He hadn't thought about any of that. It hadn't been an edict, so honestly, he'd forgotten.

"You weren't listening to us," Brodey whined. "We needed to find out what was going on."

"Yeah, and did you think maybe you could have called her up and arranged for her to come over for dinner?"

"You told us not to talk to you about her!"

"Well, you were sneaky today anyway, weren't you? What difference would it have made?"

Brodey fell silent. Ain shook his head. "Dammit."

"Maybe," Cail said, "she will want to be with us. Ever think about that?"

"How will we know? How will we know it's because she truly wants us or because now she's so fucking horny that she can't see straight?"

"Is that a bad thing?" Brodey asked.

"Goddammit!" Ain advanced, his fists clenched. "I told you I wanted a willing mate! That the old ways of taking one whether she wanted it or not were over in our line!"

"We didn't force her," Cail protested.

"You didn't give her a chance for informed consent!"

"We could tell she was the One!"

"But how is she supposed to know we're the ones for her?"

Cail and Brodey couldn't answer that.

Ain stormed out again. This time, when he hadn't returned in twenty minutes, Cail went looking for him. He found Ain's clothes on the back porch.

He'd shifted.

"Well, that conversation's over for now," he snarked, walking back inside. Yes, he'd been to plenty of ceremonies over the years where the woman was less than willing at first. But an Alpha never took a mate unless certain they were their One. Ever. And always, by the end of the ceremony, the mate—usually a woman—was happy to be taken no matter how much she protested and fought at first. Most Alphas were male, but there were a few women who took men. Like their Alpha cousin, Mary.

After attending a particularly traumatic ceremony decades earlier, Ain had swore they'd never do that. Cousins of theirs, twin Alphas, had found a woman. She'd fallen for one, the Prime, but not the other. It didn't matter, because both men knew she was their One.

And now, forty years later, the three of them were still happily together and expecting their fifteenth pup.

Cail and Brodey had missed that ceremony but it had a profound effect on Ain. He'd insisted even if it meant letting their One go, they would not force her.

But it hadn't been an edict either.

* * * *

By the end of the next afternoon, Elain was a wreck. She couldn't concentrate on anything but the memory of the feel of the Lyall brothers' tongues on her. She was about to leave for the day when her desk phone rang. She almost let it go to voice mail then decided to answer it.

"Elain Pardie."

"Hi, it's Brodey."

She closed her eyes, her sex suddenly drenched with a flood of moisture as her belly clenched. "Hi," she whispered.

"Are you okay?"

"Yeah." *If not getting you out of my mind is "okay."*

"We'd like to know if you'd please come to dinner at our place Sunday. Around seven?"

Her hand nearly crushed the receiver. A chance to see the two brothers again? *Sure!* But what about…

"I don't know if that's a good idea. I get the impression Aindreas isn't very fond of me."

"No! That's not true. He's the oldest, that's all."

Maybe not the weirdest tangent, but whatever. "You're triplets."

"It's a birth order thing. Uh, in our family, it's sort of a...tradition."

Her bullshit buzzer sounded. "Thank you for the offer but I don't think I can take you up on it." Even though the thought of refusing nearly drove her to tears.

"Please?" He sounded desperate. "Please, Elain, we'd love to have you over for dinner."

Without will of her own, she shivered. "Okay," she whispered.

* * * *

Brodey hung up and squeezed Cail in a bear hug. "She said yes!" Ain had stayed out all night running apparently, and was still gone. They were scheduled to have a Council meeting at their place on Sunday anyway, so that was perfect timing.

"Maybe by Sunday night..." Cail didn't finish, a broad grin taking over.

"I hope to hell so, brother."

Ain returned later that night. He went straight to the shower without speaking to them, then into bed. They waited an hour, until they knew he was asleep to go to bed, not wanting to disturb him.

Not wanting him to ask questions.

But Brodey and Cail were in agreement that they knew she'd want to willingly be with them. There would be no force needed for her to accept all three of them.

Chapter Five

Ain didn't speak to his brothers the next morning either. He grabbed a travel mug of coffee and headed to the barns on the other side of the property without bothering to eat breakfast.

That actually relieved Brodey and Cail. No chance for Ain to say no or cancel their plans.

Sunday morning, they left Ain asleep in bed and ran out to the store for groceries. Steak, salad, home-baked bread, a nice wine. They would have a wonderful dinner, talk with her. Surely by the end of their meal, before the Council meeting started, she'd want them as badly as they wanted her. The Council wouldn't gather until midnight. Otherwise, they'd have to wait a complete moon, till the next meeting, to mark her. Thank the Goddess at least they could mate with her before then if she didn't agree tonight.

Ain wasn't in the house when they returned, but they'd seen him in one of the fields in the work truck, taking feed out to the stock. Perfect.

By the time Ain returned to the house at six, Brodey and Cail had already showered and changed clothes. Ain sniffed the air.

"What's going on?"

Cail leveled his gaze at him. "Don't ask questions we don't want to answer, bro. Just get a shower, dress decent."

"Is she coming here?"

"Please, just do it. For once?"

Ain didn't press the issue. In a few minutes, Cail and Brodey heard the shower running in the master bath.

* * * *

Elain didn't think she could stand the wait. She had a strong suspicion she wasn't leaving the Lyall brothers' house until sometime, hopefully very late, on Monday. Fine with her, because she was so friggin' horny she could barely sit still. No matter how many times she used the shower massager or a vibrator or even her own hand, it did little more than take the rough edge off her need.

She'd never felt like this before. She was beyond the point of caring if it made her look like a slut or not, she was willing to get a little wild with those two men if they could make her feel a fraction as good as they did the other afternoon. Screw it, she was twenty-seven and had been a good girl, relatively speaking, all her life.

Time to have some fun.

She went shopping and bought herself a cute blue sundress that left nearly all of her shoulder area exposed. She imagined their lips would feel damn good kissing her there.

Forget panties. They'd be in the way.

She hoped.

No bra either.

As she looked in the mirror one final time, she realized she was dressed to get fucked.

Oh, please, God, I hope so!

She arrived at five till seven. Brodey and Cail waited for her on the porch, huge smiles on their faces.

As weird and nervous as Elain felt, she leaned in to hug them. That, however, felt right. More than right. Like she could stand there and hug them all night.

Or more. A *lot* more. Hugging them left her with a peaceful, calm feeling so strong she had to force herself to step back from their embrace.

Cail rested his hand on the small of her back and led her inside.

The old Florida ranch style house was large, the walls lined with planks of golden pecky cypress. A huge flatscreen TV hung on the wall, two large, comfortable couches and a chair in front of it, surrounding a coffee table. Large dining room table, and two hallways she assumed led off to the rest of the house.

In the large eat-in kitchen, a smaller table for four was set. Heavenly aromas assaulted her.

"We didn't put the steaks on yet," Brodey said, holding a chair out for her. "How do you like yours?"

"Rare, please."

Cail smiled. "Girl after our own hearts. I'll go put them on." He carried a plate of four steaks out a back door and she spotted a large, expensive professional-grade stainless barbeque on the outside deck.

Brodey sat next to her and took her hand. "I can't tell you how glad we are you agreed to come to dinner tonight."

She nervously smiled. Her earlier *Yippee, I'm gonna get laid!* bravado faded fast as her nerves took over. "Me too. Where's Aindreas?"

"He'll be out in a minute. Shower."

She flushed as she imagined how he looked in the shower. She had to bite back the comment, *"Does he need any help?"*

"Can I get you anything to drink?" Brodey asked. "Iced tea? Wine? Soda? Beer? Anything."

"Tea is fine." Maybe drinking wasn't a good idea. It would suck to get sick and then puke instead of having fun.

He fetched her drink. "Sugar?"

"What kind?" she purred, hoping to regain a little of the upper hand, not that she had it in the first place.

He laughed and leaned in close. She thought he'd kiss her, but he nuzzled his nose against hers. Somehow, the gesture was even more erotic.

"Whatever kind you want, baby. As much as you want."

"Yes, please!" she gasped.

He grinned and brought her the sugar bowl and a teaspoon.

They both looked up as a door opened. Aindreas' hair was still damp from the shower, and he looked damn good in khaki slacks and a button-up shirt. He walked into the kitchen and paused at the doorway. Brodey sat back. It was almost as if a silent conversation passed between the two men.

Aindreas finally spoke. "Thank you for joining us for dinner, Elain," he said.

He sounded like his brothers, and yet he didn't. His voice felt deeper, more resonant.

"Thank you for having me here tonight." *God,* please *let them have me!*

Aindreas poured himself a glass of tea and sat across the table from her. His grey eyes glittered, appraising. "I hear my brothers took you to lunch the other day."

Elain felt the deep blush in her face, wondered how much more they'd told him than that. She tried to speak, cleared her throat, licked her lips, and tried again. "Yes, they were very kind to take me out to eat." *Holy Christ, that sounded wrong.*

Aindreas smiled and hoped it wasn't too obvious how his eyes traveled her body. Goddess, she was gorgeous! As her face turned pink he struggled not to get out of his chair, sling Elain over his shoulder and carry her to bed. There was no mistaking it, they'd got it right, for once. Their One. Their mate.

If she'd have them.

No mate of his would ever beg for them to stop or plead for mercy. She would never cry in fear or scream or fight.

She would willingly want to be with them.

He prayed she would.

He briefly closed his eyes and inhaled. So close. How had she tasted? He hoped he'd get his chance soon enough. Yes, Cail and Brodey finally did something right, doing this on a Council meeting night. That would be enough time to win her over or scare her off.

Tease or not to tease? "They said they enjoyed their… conversation with you."

Brodey sat there like a moron, silently watching them talk, his head following the conversation like a tennis game.

"We had a very nice…chat."

She's feisty. "I hope you and I get to have a nice…chat later."

She flushed even deeper. His cock throbbed in his pants. Thank the Goddess he was sitting down.

"So do I," she said, finally meeting his gaze again.

He swallowed hard.

Cail returned with the steaks. "All right, four rare. Elain, let me know if yours needs more cooking." Cail dished out the meat and sat but Ain never took his eyes from Elain's, waiting for her to look away first.

She finally did with another sweet round of color rushing to her face.

Ain let the other two brothers take over the conversation for a while but he never hesitated to hold her gaze whenever she looked his way. Sweet blue eyes he could get lost in, and her shoulder-length hair perfect for him to wrap his fingers in while she sucked his cock.

Eventually she directed a comment to him. "Aindreas, do you think I could get a demonstration tonight? With the dogs?"

"That can easily be arranged." He smiled. "And feel free to call me Ain."

* * * *

It was after nine by the time they all pushed back from the table. "Where are your dogs anyway?" Elain asked. She wished Beta was inside so she could say hi to him.

"They're outside in the barn tonight. Didn't want them begging." He looked at his brothers. "Why don't you two go out there and get them ready? We'll be along in a few minutes."

Cail and Brodey nodded and walked out the back door.

Leaving her alone with Ain. He stood and offered his hand. Her heart raced in her chest as she laced her fingers through his.

What *was* it about these three gorgeous guys? What was their game? Part of her instinctively knew she shouldn't be doing this but she was past the point of caring. If men could play around, why couldn't women?

When he pulled her into his arms she offered no resistance. He kissed her. His tongue gently traced and parted the seam of her lips and she pressed her body against his. Something in his touch also soothed her, calmed her, made her feel better than she had over the past few days. When he lifted his face from hers he smiled, but it looked sad.

"What's wrong?" she asked.

"You're wonderful."

"You guys don't get out much, do you?"

He laughed and stepped away, much to her regret. He took her hand. "Let's go."

Two of the dogs were in the barn, sitting, waiting. Cail and Brodey were nowhere to be seen. Apparently this barn was mostly for equipment and storage and offices, because there were no stalls or horses or cows inside and the concrete floor looked relatively clean. She pet Beta, happy to see him. He happily whined as she scratched him behind the ears. Gamma nudged her hand and she pet him, too. Both dogs eagerly rubbed against her legs.

"Shouldn't we wait for your brothers?" she asked.

Ain shrugged, leading her through the barn to a large corral behind it. It was dark outside but the corral was well-lit. Inside, a small flock of about fifteen sheep huddled by the back fence.

"They probably went to check on something." He turned to the dogs. "Beta, Gamma, walk up."

The two dogs squeezed through the rail fence and walked out to the flock, then stopped, waiting.

"Normally in competition," Ain explained, casually leaning against the fence, "there are a bunch of things you have to do with the flock, specific patterns, drive gates, pens, things like that." He looked at the dogs. "Lift."

Moving as a carefully choreographed unit, both dogs slowly circled the sheep, gently nudging them away from the fence without breaking their huddled group.

"There are specific commands we use for competition. Here in a working setting, especially dealing with cattle, we don't always use those exact commands. These sheep are only for training and exhibition. Normally the dogs are working cattle." He looked at the dogs. "Away to me," he called out.

The dogs began moving the sheep around the pen in a counter-clockwise direction. When they were almost at their original starting point, Ain called out, "Look back!"

Both dogs stopped and looked at him.

"Come-bye." The dogs worked the sheep around the pen clockwise. At the starting point again, Ain called out, "Look back!"

The dogs stopped and did, waiting.

"Beta, shed two. Gamma, hold the rest."

Elain looked at him. "You're kidding?"

He smiled. "Nope. Watch."

Sure enough, the green-eyed dog split two sheep off the end and carefully drove them toward the gate where Elain and Ain stood. Gamma kept the rest of the sheep in a tightly balled mass toward the back corral fence.

When Beta had the sheep in front of them, Ain called out, "Send 'em back." Beta circled around and started the sheep toward the flock. Gamma stepped away and allowed them to rejoin the group. "That'll do." Both dogs trotted back to Ain and sat, waiting.

He turned to her. "It's more impressive when it's a hundred head of cows that weigh nearly a thousand pounds each."

"I bet. How many cows do you have?"

"Right now, we've got nearly two thousand head. We raise and ship high-end breed stock all over the country. That part of the operation is based on the other side of the property, away from the house. We like our privacy. Our employees use the other gate."

They returned to the barn, the dogs following. She walked alongside Ain. When her hand brushed his, a thrill ran through her as his fingers gripped hers. The other two brothers were still nowhere to be seen.

Somehow, she had a feeling that was planned. Whether by them or by Ain or all three in cahoots, she didn't know yet.

She didn't care.

The dogs sat and stared at them as Ain pulled her into his arms. "Why did you come here tonight," he hoarsely asked.

She felt his rock-hard erection through his slacks. "Because your brother asked me to."

"But why did you accept?"

His grey eyes pierced into hers. She couldn't lie. "Because I wanted to see what would happen," she whispered.

He kissed her, crushing her lips, holding her body tightly against his.

More than happy to let go and give herself to him, she softly moaned into his mouth as one of his hands gripped her ass and he ground his hips into her.

As suddenly as it started, he practically pushed her away. He stepped back, nearly tripping over the dogs. "I can't do it like this."

She took a step toward him. "Do what? Like what?"

He grabbed her hands. "We need to talk to you. Tell you some things. All three of us want you."

She nodded, mustered her courage. "I'm willing to have a wild weekend with you boys. I'm beyond caring what it makes me look like. Did your brothers tell you about the other day?"

"You don't understand—"

"I don't care! I won't tell if you won't. I know it'll just be for fun.

I won't ask any of you guys for anything, just a really hot night. I'm on the Pill, I brought some condoms if you don't have any, so let's play."

He looked at the dogs. "Shift."

"What?" She did a double-take as the two large black dogs suddenly turned into Cailean and Brodey before her eyes.

The air exploded out of her lungs.

Chapter Six

Ain reached for Elain's hand as she stumbled. He grabbed a saddle blanket and led her to a nearby bale of hay, guiding her to sit. Her eyes looked wide as she stared at the two naked men sitting on the floor before her.

Ain stepped back and started unbuttoning his shirt. "We've got a pretty big secret. I don't know where to begin."

She stared, speechless.

He looked at his brothers. "Back."

They were two black dogs again.

"How...what...how..."

"Shape-shifters," he said, removing his shirt. He kicked off his shoes. His slacks were next, he hadn't bothered with underwear and his stiff cock sprung free as he stripped.

Elain's brain tried and failed to process what she'd just witnessed. Ain had stripped—holy Christ his cock was gorgeous!—and changed into a dog, then back.

"I'm the Prime Alpha." Ain watched her shocked look grow even wider as he walked to stand in front of her.

She stared at him.

"You aren't dreaming, and we didn't drug you. This is real."

Elain stared, speechless. *What the holy fuck?*

"We're over two hundred and thirty years old," he said. "Long story short, shape-shifters aren't a myth. And you're our One."

"One what?" she whispered, not sure of her voice.

"The One. For us. Mate."

That broke through her shock. "Huh?"

He knelt before her and took her hands. His face softened. Something in her wanted to reach out and hold him. "We've never found our One before. Alpha shifters mate for life. Which is pretty long, if you haven't guessed. It's not like the movies, you have to be born one to actually change. When we take a mate, it changes them in some ways, too. A non-shifter mate takes on a lot of their shifter mate's power. Or mates'—plural—in this case. Most shifters are male."

"Whoa!" She looked at them. "All three of you?"

He playfully smiled. "I thought you said you wanted some fun."

"I...I do...I did...what the fuck?"

He gently pulled her to him and kissed her. She felt the resistance melt from her body at his touch. When his hand slid under her dress, Elain moaned, wanting more.

He pushed back the fabric and dipped his head between her legs. When his tongue gently swiped at her clit she felt reality loosen and her world exploded after only seconds. She cried out as the unquenchable ache she'd felt ever since the parking lot adventure was at least temporarily sated.

The other two brothers shifted to men again and gathered close. She stared at them, wondering if she'd just lost her mind.

Ain looked at her. "I can't—we can't do more unless or until you agree to be our mate. I will not force you."

She already felt the urgent throbbing start again, wanting release, needing them. "Yes!"

He shook his head. "You don't understand. You would be ours, forever. Only ours. All three of us."

Elain looked at their faces. Brodey and Cail looked desperately hopeful. Ain looked sad.

His words suddenly broke through her sexual haze.

"Forever?" she asked.

He nodded. Releasing her hand, he sat back. "We mate for life.

You would have to quit your job—"

That got her attention. "Whoa!" She sat up and pulled her dress down. "What? Quit my *job*? It took me three years to make it from photojournalist to on-air. I'm not quitting!" She decided to hold off on trying to process the other crazy bullshit for a few minutes. One thing at a time or her brain would fry. *This* she could handle.

Ain nodded. "Okay. There's more, but if that's a deal-breaker then there's no use explaining it." He stood and picked up his clothes. She looked at the other two men and started to reach for them but they sadly stood and backed away.

"Wait!" She looked up at them. "We can't just play?"

Ain shook his head. "It doesn't work like that. When we meet our One, you can't undo it once you consummate. And I won't force you to be with us if you don't want to be." He pulled on his slacks. He carefully tucked his stiff cock inside as he zipped them.

"What?"

"I'm sorry, Elain. You are the One for us. I refuse to take a mate unless she's totally willing."

"Why can't we just play?" she asked again. The need had returned with a vengeance, quickly taking away her ability to think straight, much less speak.

"It doesn't work like that."

Rage set in. "So you…what…hypnotize me to make me think something weird's going on, get me all fucking hot to trot and leave me hanging?"

His wry smile only served to piss her off more. "I just got you off. We're the ones left hanging." The other two men were also stiff. They'd retrieved clothes and were pulling them on.

"This is crazy!"

"I know. It's hard to believe. The old ways were when an Alpha shifter found his One, he took her, regardless of whether she was attracted to him or not. Once it was consummated she felt it too because of their connection. I won't do that. I can't do that." He turned away from her. "I'm sorry."

"Sorry?" She didn't know what else to say.

"It'll take a few weeks before you start to feel normal, probably. Hopefully."

Weeks? If she stayed as horny as she'd been for the next few weeks she'd end up in the hospital.

She angrily stood. "Oh, no you *fucking* don't!" She pointed at Cail and Brodey. "You two assholes did something to me the other day and now I can't seem to feel anything but horny! What the fuck did you do?"

Ain nodded again. "That's because you feel it. You feel the connection too. I'm sorry." They'd almost finished dressing.

This felt like a good time for a temper tantrum. "No. Fucking. Way! You assholes do NOT get to leave me feeling like this with a simple, 'I'm sorry,' bullshit excuse!"

"If you become our mate, that feeling would go away, being with us. We will kill and die for you, love and protect you. Spend our lives doing nothing but trying to make you happy, spoiling you rotten, and I mean that literally. But you have to submit to the Alpha. I know it sounds like bullshit, but it's a shifter thing. We're bound by the Code. In this case, we're triplets, we're all Alphas. So you have to submit especially to the Prime."

"You?"

He nodded.

Love? That word belatedly hit her brain. "How the fuck can you say you love me? You don't even know me."

"You're our One. We can't not love you. You would complete us." He turned to leave the barn.

"Where are you going?"

"Inside to clean up the kitchen. We have to do the dishes." The other brothers started to follow him.

"You've *got* to be shitting me? You're walking away?"

Ain turned. "Then submit," he softly said. "That's all you have to do."

She stared at him. The whole crazy shape-shifter stuff was trying to bubble its way to the surface but so was the incredible, aching need deep in her belly.

"Why? Why do I have to do that?"

"It's a shifter thing. I'm sorry. We don't make the rules."

"You're what, asking me to be your personal love slave?"

His eyes blazed. "No! We're asking for the chance to love and cherish and protect you for the rest of our lives."

Part of her wanted to drop to her knees right then and beg him to take her. Like the other afternoon when he ordered his brothers into the house, she'd wanted to follow. A deep craving she couldn't explain, a primal urge.

Her brain, however, rebelled against the concept.

"I can't," she said, near tears as her inner conflict threatened to rip her soul apart.

He nodded and sadly smiled. "I understand." He turned and walked toward the house.

She stood there in the barn, staring at them. *No. Fucking. Way!*

Hypnosis? Date rape drug? Well, maybe not date rape because they didn't fuck her. But what the hell?

Rage washed through her. She stomped down the path after them, catching Ain's arm on the front porch. She spun him around. "You mean to tell me, beyond the crazy bullshit I'm still not sure how you pulled off, that I'm standing here *begging* all of you to fuck me and you won't?"

He crossed his arms. "The second you say you agree, we'll carry you to bed and make love to you all night long. But in submitting, you are agreeing to be ours. We will not force you."

"Uh, isn't that force, telling me I'd have to quit my job? What the fuck? How do I even know I'd like you assholes in the morning, much less want to spend 'forever'"—she used finger quotes—"with you?"

"You would. Just like we know we'd still love you in the morning."

"Oh, because I'm 'the One?'" More finger quotes.

He nodded. "Exactly."

"Okay. For shits and giggles, tell me this. What else would happen?"

"There's a Council meeting tonight, in a couple of hours. They would verify the mating and witness the marking—"

"Whoa! Time out!" She stepped back. "You're talking *group* sex?" Of course, that's what she was already thinking before, but only with the triplets.

"No. When Alpha shifters take a mate and mark them, the Council witnesses the marking. It's different for twins, and of course us, than for just two people. There's normally no need for the Council to verify the mating when it's a single shifter, only the marking. When more than one shifter is involved in the mating, they need to verify all have been joined before the mate is marked.

She stared at him, her mouth gaping. *Okay, mental overload. Brain officially, totally fried.*

She stormed past him into the house, grabbed her purse, and back out again. Not fast enough to miss the heartbroken looks on Cail and Brodey's faces. Elain stopped on the front porch, where Ain still stood. "Why can't I play with those two instead of you?"

He shook his head. "It has to be all. And Prime has to be first."

Figures. "Asshat!" It sounded lame but was all she could think of. She stomped to her car, slammed the door shut, then sat staring at Ain. He stood on the porch, watching her.

Crazy to the Nth degree. Creepy voyeuristic shape-shifting men getting their jollies watching…

"ARRRRGGGHHHH!" she screamed, punched her steering wheel. The ache between her legs was a full-blown cramping wave she couldn't ignore.

Ain stood on the porch and watched her.

She started the car, turned around, and drove toward the road. By the time she reached Highway 17 fifteen minutes later, where it intersected downtown Arcadia, Elain had to pull over and curl into a ball on the seat. Between crying and her body's desperate need, she couldn't go any further.

"FUUUUUCK!" she screamed as she lay on her side and kicked at the door. What had those bastards done to her?

Something, that's for sure, because she'd never felt like this before. The memory of Ain's hand around hers, his arms around her, the feel of Cail and Brodey's hands and lips and tongues...

Those were the only thoughts that brought her the slightest bit of comfort or relief.

The word *submit* ran through her brain and something about it soothed a part of her soul.

No!

She'd worked too hard to give up her life for three hard bodies.

Three hard bodies who seemed to want her, only her.

She sat there for a long time, crying, screaming, thinking.

Aching.

It was nearly eleven.

Ain walked onto the front porch when she drove up. He didn't move, didn't come to greet her.

She sat there and stared at him through the windshield for another five minutes before taking a deep breath and getting out. Driving toward the house, her discomfort had somewhat lessened but it still felt damn bad.

Elain walked up to the porch. "What do you mean by submit?"

"Prime is in charge. That's the way it is. We're all Alpha."

"I mean, do you pimp your women out?"

Even in the dim light from the porch fixture she saw his face redden in rage. "I would kill any man who dared touch you."

She smirked. "What about your brothers?"

"You know what I mean."

"No, I don't! That's the *fucking* point! You're asking me to promise you forever when I hardly know you and I can barely think, when it feels like someone's fucking twisting my clit and my guts into knots and springing crazy shifter shit on me that I'm still not sure I believe, but...*fuck!*" She hadn't planned on crying again, but she did. She dropped to her knees and sobbed.

Ain didn't move toward her. His voice softened even more. "Elain, I am so sorry it happened like this. I really am. This is what I did not want to happen. I never wanted you to feel any discomfort. I wanted you to fall in love with us and want to be with us willingly, not because you felt compelled to. I swore that we would not force our mate, if we found her, to be with us. I failed to realize my stupid brothers wouldn't think about the consequences of their actions with you the other day."

He knelt to meet her teary gaze but didn't move from the porch. "We will love you and protect you and take care of you. We will never cheat on you. We will cherish you and do whatever we can that's in our power to make you happy, we are bound by the Code to ensure your happiness. Honestly? I seriously meant it when I said we will spoil you rotten. But the one thing—the only thing—we ask in return is you have to submit to us."

"Why can't I keep my job?"

"Because for one, it's hard to keep a low profile in TV. If you were in nearly any other profession, I would let you make the decision. For another, most mates don't want to work outside the home."

"What, get me barefoot and pregnant?" she bitterly spat.

The thought of her belly round with his child made Ain's cock throb again. "Not like that. It's like we wouldn't want to be that far from you for any length of time. Or you from us. It's practically a physical need, to be with your mate."

"But you want kids."

"Eventually." That was the truth. "Not right now if you don't want them. If you decided you never wanted kids, we wouldn't force you. We will never force you. That's totally up to you." Frankly, he wanted years to play with her and knew his brothers did, too. They'd have many years to have pups, if she wanted them. It didn't have to be right now.

"So, you're not worried about me saying no and leaving and telling people what you are?"

He smiled wryly. "I can see that conversation going well. 'Hey, let's go film these guys turning into wolves.'"

She froze, then sobbed again. "I'm losing my fucking mind."

He wanted to go to her, hold her, console her. He couldn't.

"If it's any comfort, trust me, you'd be getting your way around here most of the time. We would treat you like a princess, sweetheart. I promise."

Apparently it wasn't a comfort, because she sobbed harder.

He was aware of Cail and Brodey stepping out the front door. He silently warned them not to touch her. He was also aware of the Council members drawing close. They were expecting ten tonight, ones who lived in the area.

Ain stood. "We can make you feel better," he softly said. "Or you can wait it out and in a few weeks it'll probably be bearable, if not better. Then you won't have to quit your job. It would break our hearts, and we would hate like hell to lose you but I will not force you to choose us. We only want to make you happy."

He motioned his brothers to go inside. He stood and followed them, gently shutting the door on the sound of her sobbing.

Brodey looked near tears, as did Cail. "We can't leave her out there like that," Cail said. "Dammit, she's a wreck!"

Ain's face hardened. "It's you two's fault, asshole. You did this to her. This is what I did *not* want to happen. Thanks to you, she's in misery right now."

"Well, you sure as hell didn't hesitate to sample the goodies out there in the barn earlier," Brodey angrily shot back.

Ain hated himself for that, too. "It didn't make matters worse. You'd already done the damage. At least it gave her a few minutes of relief."

The sound of the door opening startled them. Elain stood in the doorway, tears running down her face. She threw herself at Ain. He caught her and she wrapped her arms and legs around him as she kissed him.

Brodey kicked the door shut and followed them into the living room. Ain tried to set her on the couch but she wouldn't let go. He turned and sat and she ground her hips against his.

"Please," she begged. "Please make it stop. Anything, just please make me feel better."

He finally peeled her arms from around his neck and held her wrists firmly clamped in his hands. "Look at me, Elain," he said.

She met his gaze.

"Us and only us. And you will be the only woman we are ever with, ever again." She was so beautiful. Their One.

She nodded.

Chapter Seven

She'd agree to anything short of murder to make this unscratchable itch go away for good. She felt Ain's stiff cock between her legs as she rubbed herself against his slacks.

"You must agree to willingly submit to us," he said. "We swear to spend our lives making you happy, we promise."

She nodded. "Wait, what about protection?"

"You're on the Pill?"

She nodded.

"Shifter perk. No STDs. But if you want, we'll use something."

"No." She wanted this feeling gone. Now.

He kissed her and she was vaguely aware of him reaching between them, pulling up her dress and unzipping his slacks. Then his hard cock slid inside her and she gasped, shuddering.

Gone. The worst was gone.

She sobbed with relief and closed her eyes as she dropped her head to Ain's shoulder. Vaguely aware of Brodey on one side and Cail on the other, she didn't care whose hands were where as Ain fucked his huge cock inside her. One of them found her clit and rubbed it. Someone else reached inside her dress and pinched and rolled her nipples in their fingers. When she cried out as she climaxed, she heard Ain grunt with satisfaction. He grabbed her hips and pounded into her several times before she felt him coming inside her.

Peace. A warm, relaxing cloud settled over her. After days of unrequited agitation, it was almost like the world's best beer buzz.

Submission gooooood.

They didn't move, didn't speak. Ain's hands gently stroked her back while Brodey and Cail each curled an arm around her shoulders. After a few minutes Ain stood, still holding her, his cock still inside her, and carried her into their bedroom.

She kept her eyes closed but felt him gently lay her on a bed. The mattress dipped as the other brothers knelt on either side of her. Then Ain kissed her and she knew regardless of what would happen, this had been the right decision.

He withdrew, leaving her slightly sad and empty. She opened her eyes and watched him remove his clothes. Apparently Cail and Brodey had stripped on the way into the bedroom because they were already naked. They lifted her dress up and over her head, and each bent to take a nipple into their mouth.

She closed her eyes again and moaned. Brodey released her breast, then she felt more movement on the bed. She cracked an eyelid open and Brodey and Ain had switched position. *Jeezus pleezus, they were identical like this, too.*

Brodey lined up his cock with her ready sex and said, "Look at me, babe."

Unable to resist, she did.

Slowly, almost torturously slow, he pressed in until his pubic bone rubbed against her clit. He softly groaned. "Do you want me to fuck you, baby?" he hoarsely asked.

She nodded.

He lifted her legs over his shoulders and stroked his cock into her, driving deep, filling her.

Ain lifted his head from her breast as his fingers stroked her clit. "Come for us, baby," he whispered. "We want another one from you. We're going to make up for what you went through, we promise."

She threw her head back and moaned. Everything they did felt right. Never before had she felt like this. He gently pinched her clit in time with his brother's strokes. Before long she felt another climax start.

Brodey's last several strokes drove hard and deep and he moaned with her as he finished. Panting, he carefully lowered her legs and kissed the base of her throat. "Beautiful," he murmured. "You're so beautiful."

After a few minutes, Brodey withdrew and Cail switched places with him. He stroked her thighs and slipped inside her, stretching his legs along hers, holding his weight on his arms. At that angle, every stroke he took deliciously slid along her throbbing clit in a way the other two hadn't.

With Ain and Brodey gently biting her nipples, Elain gave up trying to help. She tangled her fingers in Ain and Brodey's hair and closed her eyes and enjoyed the overwhelming sensation. Cail seemed to last forever. When she was about to suggest he go ahead and enjoy himself, a deep, burning tingle started between her legs and she realized she was about to come again.

"Fuck!" she screamed, tightly gripping the other men's hair, bucking her hips against Cail.

He waited a second, then finished, dropping to lie on top of her, his head on her chest.

She let go of Ain and Brodey and wrapped her arms around Cail. Drifting off to sleep looked like a damn good option at this point. She knew she'd be sore in a good way in the morning, but the damned unscratchable erotic itch was gone.

So was her heart.

These men owned it, and she knew it. It didn't make sense, it sounded trite and stupid, but she knew it was the truth.

They lay there for a few minutes when Ain lifted his head. "Shit. Council in fifteen." He sat up. "Shower."

Elain didn't want to move. Fuck the Council. She wanted to lie there and go to sleep with her men.

Her men!

That would take some getting used to.

Cail kissed her and got up. Then she felt one of them—Ain, it turned out—pick her up and carry her.

"Sorry, baby, but we need to clean you up." One of the other men started the shower and when Ain tried to put her down, she kept her arms wrapped around his neck.

He laughed, a sound that twisted her heart in a good way. "This won't take long, then we'll come back here and sleep until next week if you want. How's that sound?"

"Promise?"

Cail nudged in next to her. It amazed her she could already tell them apart that much, his voice sounded slightly softer than his brothers, and his scent was subtly different. "Absolutely." Cail soaped a washcloth and scrubbed her down while Brodey nuzzled the back of her neck.

Between the three men they quickly got her cleaned up and out of the shower in less than five minutes, although all three looked stiff and ready for another round.

Ain had a large, fluffy towel ready for her. He wrapped it around her and held her, nuzzled her ear. "Trust us. Please. No one will touch you but us, I promise. Pretend it's just the three of us."

That sliced through her mellow like a chainsaw through warm butter. "What?"

"It'll only take a few minutes. Please, trust us."

She swallowed hard but nodded. What the hell had she agreed to? Now with one problem solved, reality came knocking.

When she was dry, Ain handed her the sundress and she slipped it over her head. She thought the men would get dressed but they didn't, walking naked with her to the front door.

"What do I do?" she said.

"Just follow me," Ain said. "Do what we say." He stopped and turned to her. "This is an ancient ceremony. We have to do things a certain way. We can't change it. I promise we won't hurt you, but you have to trust us." He kissed her and she fought the urge to melt against him.

She didn't bother to put her shoes on. She followed them down the path to the barn. Inside were ten of the largest dogs—except for the guys—she'd ever seen in her life. Most looking like wolf hybrids of some sort.

Gathered in a large, loose semi-circle, they made no sound, intently watched.

Brodey had been carrying a blanket and something else that looked like a small plastic bottle. He spread the blanket on the floor in the middle of the semi-circle. Suddenly, the three men shifted into dogs again.

Elain swallowed hard. *Oh boy.*

Ain's grey eyes nailed her. She was aware of Brodey and Cail somewhere behind her, but she wasn't sure where. Ain sat in front of her on the blanket and looked at her. A low, rumbling growl started deep in his throat. She realized all three were doing it. They stopped.

She wasn't sure what she was supposed to do.

All the other dogs growled. *Oh, yeah, right, like I can ignore THAT and pretend they aren't there.*

When they fell silent, all were still.

Ain stood and walked forward.

He growled again, only different. In her mind, his soft voice whispered.

Submit.

Her heart raced. She glanced behind her, but the other two brothers lowered their heads and rumbled again.

She turned back to Ain. Closing her eyes, she sank to her knees.

Soft chuffing sounds from the other dogs. Shifters? Wolves? What the fuck was she supposed to call them other than canine perverts? *Whatever*, apparently she'd done the right thing.

Ain stepped forward and lifted his head. She wasn't sure what to do, so she crouched on the blanket on her hands and knees. *Please, God, let 'em shift back before they do anything. I don't care what they are, I don't want to do it with a dog!*

She felt Ain's warm, dense fur along her neck and shoulders, then her heart nearly stopped as something firm gripped the back of her neck, pointed but not so hard that it hurt.

Teeth.

Another soft, rumbling growl.

She felt gentle pressure as he pushed down.

Elain lowered herself to the blanket, ass in the air, and closed her eyes as the pressure released. Then his fur again, pressing against her, standing over her. He growled, echoed by Cail and Brodey.

Our mate, the soft mental voice whispered.

The others chuffed.

Then he was gone. She didn't look. *Okay, that wasn't so bad.*

She felt a hand stroke her ass through the dress. *Whew! Okay, definitely not bad.* She dared look and saw Ain kneeling behind her. Brodey and Cail had also shifted back. Brodey knelt in front of her while Cail stood to his side. Ain lifted her dress and she closed her eyes again. This would be a lot easier, whatever happened, without the other eyes on her, even if they were dogs.

The other two men helped pull her dress off. She heard a soft noise and looked again, saw Ain had the bottle Brodey had carried.

Aw, crap. Lube.

And sure enough, he pressed a lubed finger against her virgin rim. That's when she started to sit up and he placed a firm hand in the middle of her back as she looked over her shoulder at him.

"Please," he whispered. His eyes pleaded with her.

"I've never...not there," she whispered. "Please, no."

The firm hand became gentle, stroking. "You have to submit," he whispered. "We have to do this."

Two hands closed over hers and she looked. Cail and Brodey laced their fingers through hers. "Please," Brodey whispered, so softly she suspected even the other whatevers couldn't hear.

Cail nuzzled her forehead, gently kissed her. "It's okay, babe," he whispered.

She dropped her head to the blanket and tried not to cry from embarrassment. It didn't hurt, but she damn sure didn't want her first time like this to be in front of a bunch of strange mutts.

Ain gently worked lube into her, still stroking her back with his free hand. Then she felt his fingers withdraw and a moment later, more lube and two fingers pressed for entrance. She tried to bite back her nervous moan, but she couldn't.

He hesitated, waiting.

After a few minutes he worked up to three fingers and she tried not to tense when she knew what was next. His large cock pressed against her and she froze, afraid. He waited, stroking her back, then curled around her.

"Breathe," he whispered into her ear. "Relax." He finally pressed through the first resistance and waited for her to adjust.

It was hard to breathe and relax, especially with the uncomfortable burn in her ass as his cock stretched her, but she did her best. After a moment he slowly pressed forward until he was fully sheathed inside her.

Then his strong arms encircled her. He sat up, pulling her against his chest, her head against his shoulder. He tenderly kissed her cheek. "Relax, sweetie," he whispered.

She was aware of Brodey crowding close in front of them. When she felt his cock between her legs she realized what was happening.

Ain felt her tense. "Relax," he whispered. "Please."

Fighting back a sob, she relaxed in his arms.

Having Brodey slide inside her erotically stretched her, filling her with sensations she'd never had before. When he started playing with her nipples, the little remaining discomfort soon transformed to pleasure.

She gasped, panting. Ain slid one hand lower, between her legs, and found her clit. She moaned.

Okay, that was damn *good.*

A gentle hand caressed her cheek. She opened her eyes and Cail stood there, looking down at her, his stiff cock...

Oh boy.

She met his eyes and he nodded.

Why not? Hell, maybe she'd wake up with food poisoning in the hospital or something and this would all have been a dream. She closed her eyes and reached for him, pulled him to her. She wrapped her lips around his cock and enjoyed the soft, deep rumbling that swept through his body.

Well, damn. *He must like that.*

He gently fisted her hair and she gave up trying to think or even hold herself up. Her men were in control, taking her along for the ride.

Ain gently nipped her ear. "Come for us, baby," he whispered. "Please."

She was about to tell him there was no way in hell she'd ever make it when she felt it start, shocking her, then ripping a loud cry from her lips, muffled by Cail's cock in her mouth. As she came she suddenly felt Ain's teeth clamp down hard on her right shoulder, breaking the skin probably, but that only served to drive her further and faster over the edge. Then all three men were moving, thrusting, groaning. She tasted Cail as his seed pumped over her tongue and didn't even have time to consider the taste—not bad, actually—before another blast of her own hit her, rocking her, setting off explosions behind her eyelids.

All strength gone, she went limp in their arms and trusted they would hold her. She winced slightly as Ain and Brodey withdrew. One of them, Ain, lowered her to the blanket and protectively curled his body around her, holding her tightly against him.

Then Brodey snuggled in tight on her other side while Cail stroked her hair.

Exhausted, she dozed.

She awoke to being carried, wrapped in the blanket, in Ain's arms. She closed her eyes again. If they needed her, they'd say so.

She heard them walk through the house, then she smelled chlorine and heard water rumbling.

Ain kissed her forehead. "Let's sit in the hot tub for a little while, baby," he whispered.

She nodded.

He set her on her feet but kept one arm around her, unswaddled her from the blanket, then picked her up and stepped in. She heard the other two men get in but she didn't open her eyes, content to stay curled tightly against Ain's chest in the comfortably warm water.

Hands tenderly stroked her arms, held her hands, rubbed her feet. She'd be...well, fucking sore in the morning. All over. She had no idea how long they sat there because she kept dozing off. As exhausted as she was, physically, mentally, and emotionally, she also felt safer and more secure than she ever had in her entire life.

A gentle finger touched her lips. "Open, sweetie. Take these." She thought that was Cail. He popped two capsules into her mouth, followed by a straw. She swallowed the medicine, then drank the cold water, all without opening her eyes.

"Tylenol PM," he said. *Yep, definitely Cail*, she thought. His voice bore a softer edge than the other two.

She snuggled against Ain's chest again and drifted. At one point she felt them swaddle her in a towel, was aware of the men talking, and then the feel of cool, crisp sheets against her skin. Ain's warm, firm body protectively curled around her.

She slept.

Chapter Eight

When Elain opened her eyes, she instinctively snuggled tightly against the warm, firm body pressed into her back.

Ain.

She knew it without looking, although she wasn't sure how.

He kissed the back of her neck and pulled her closer. "How do you feel?" The deeper quality of his voice confirmed her suspected identification.

She was afraid to move too much. Starting with her toes, she carefully wiggled and stretched parts. Her leg muscles, especially her thighs, offered up a protest, and she was a little raw around the edges, so to speak, but nothing she couldn't deal with. Her shoulder ached where he'd bit her. Overall she felt like she'd been twisted into a pretzel, stretched, then put together inside out by someone reading the human being assembly instruction manual backwards.

Other than that, damn spiffy.

"I'll live."

"But will you enjoy it?"

She laughed and carefully rolled over to face him. His playful smile made her heart thump. Yep, she had it bad for him. "I think so." The blinds were drawn but she saw it was daylight outside from the way sunlight struggled to peek around the edges. They were alone in the bedroom. She realized it was a huge freaking bed, and the bedroom door was shut.

"What time is it?"

"Nearly noon." He brushed his fingers along her cheek. "Are you really okay? Want me to get you more Tylenol or something?"

"Not right now. I'm too comfy for you to move."

"Then I'll stay right here." He pressed a kiss to her temple.

She closed her eyes again and relaxed. "Where are the others?"

"I made them pull their weight today. They're doing chores. I usually run the outside end of the operation. Cail handles the office stuff, Brodey does whatever we tell him to do."

"It's good ta be da Prime, huh?"

He laughed. The deep, rumbling sound stirred her insides even though she was still too damn tired to do anything about it. "Yeah, it does have its perks sometimes."

"I don't know anything about you," she softly said. Awake and without the horribly debilitating horniness, now she could think straight.

"Ask."

"Anything?"

"Anything."

She tipped her head back to look into his eyes. "Where were you born?"

"Outside of Aberdeen." The way he said it, he rolled the R a little and her breath caught in her throat.

"Not the one over in Palm Beach?"

He laughed and shook his head. "Not even close."

"You guys are Scottish? Like, from Scotland Scottish?"

He grinned. "Aye, lass."

"Holy crap!" she breathlessly said.

"What?"

"Say some more!"

"Some more what?"

"Talk like that!"

He laughed and rolled onto his back. "Baby, please don't ask us to quote *Braveheart*. I'm so sick of that movie I could scream." He looked at her. "We spent a lot of years learning to not speak with a brogue when we came to the States. Then after we left Maine, it took me nearly ten years to quit saying *ayuh* when we moved here to Florida."

She pouted.

"Oh, honey, do *not* pull the puppy dog eyes on me this fast," he chided. "Give me a day or so."

"How long have you been in Florida?"

"We moved here in 1948."

Okay, now was the time to start dealing with the crazy shape-shifter stuff. She carefully, with his help, sat up. "What's going to happen to me now?"

He propped himself up on one arm. Elain tried not to stare at his firm abs. "You mean by being our mate?"

"Yeah."

"You felt the first thing last night. Being able to hear us with your mind. But it'll take a while to kick in full-time. Usually several weeks, if not months."

"So that was real?"

He nodded.

"What else?"

"Aging slows way down. Beyond that we'll have to wait and see. It's different for every mate. Being with three Alphas, it could mean you become pretty strong in some ways."

She needed a moment to come to terms with all of that. The previous night felt fuzzy, hazy in her mind. "I thought there could only be one Alpha in a family."

"Pack," he gently corrected.

"Pack. Why do you three live together?"

"Triplets. It's different. We're identical."

"No you're not. Your eyes are different."

"For all intents and purposes we're identical. If you have two brothers who are different ages and both Alpha, good luck getting them to live together long term in the same house. It won't happen. We're the only known triplets. There are some twins, but even with twins sometimes only one's a shifter. When that's the case, they usually don't live together. Or if one's an Alpha and one isn't, even if they're both shifters, they can have separate mates. There are very few twin shifters where both are Alpha. Then they have to live together to find their One. In multiple litters, the Alpha shifters have to share their One."

She studied his face. "Why did you make me do that last night, up the ass? I'm not happy that my first time was like that."

He reddened and looked away. "I'm sorry. It was part of the ceremony. I told you, they had to verify the mating. We won't ever make you do that again if you don't want to."

She might want to, but not in front of an audience and certainly not in the next few days until her body recovered from last night's lupine Lambada. She snorted. "Thank God you weren't quadruplets."

He snickered. "Yeah, that would have made things logistically challenging. At least with twins you get a little choice how to do it." He met her eyes, looked worried. "Are you really okay?"

"Physically, yeah, I'll be okay. Mentally I'm still…adjusting."

He leaned in and brushed a tender kiss across her lips. "We should go down to the courthouse tomorrow and get married—"

"Whoa!" She pushed him back. "Stop right the fuck there!"

"What?"

"You're making me quit my job *and* you're just going to fucking drag me down to the courthouse to get married? Are you shitting me?"

He frowned. "We need to work on your mouth, too."

She threw back the covers despite the pain it caused her and climbed out of bed. She didn't see her dress but a T-shirt hung from the closet doorknob. She pulled it on and it fell nearly to her knees.

"Where are you going?"

She stomped to the door. "This is my daily temper tantrum. I guess if I'm your One you'll just have to learn to fucking live with it." She flung the bedroom door open, but before she was halfway through the living room Ain had his arm around her waist and had tossed her over his shoulder like she weighed nothing.

"No you don't, babe. You're not leaving here like that."

She started thrashing and kicking and realized it was like pounding on a tree. Back to the bedroom. He kicked the door shut behind him and dumped her on the bed. "You aren't going anywhere until you've had time to recover. You need your rest."

She tried to get up and he knelt over her.

"Let me go!"

He pinned her to the bed and fixed his gaze on her. "*Stop*," he said, his voice deep and coming from somewhere powerful.

All will drained from her. *Fuck!*

He softened his voice. "Elain, honey, please. Just *calm down*. Don't go off half-cocked."

Despite not wanting to cry, she did. "Dammit, this is not fair!"

"I never said you couldn't have a wedding," he calmly said.

"You said we were going to the courthouse!"

"You never asked if that was negotiable. That was my *idea*, not a final decree. A rational person would have said, 'But I don't want to get married at the courthouse.' And I would have said, 'Then what *do* you want to do?' And a rational person would have said…" His voice drifted off. He looked at her, and she realized he was waiting for her to fill in the blank.

In a soft voice she barely recognized as her own, she said, "I want a real wedding."

He leaned in and kissed her, then released her hands and sat up. "Okay. That's progress. This is a two-way street, you know."

"Well, maybe a rational man would have said, 'Honey, I'd like to get married at the courthouse, but what do you want to do?'"

He thought about it and nodded. "You're right."

She blinked. "What?"

"You're right. I'm sorry."

She blinked again. "Huh?"

He smiled. "I'm sorry. I apologize. You're right that after what happened last night, that probably came out sounding wrong."

She stared at him in disbelief. "You're apologizing? That easy?"

"Um, yeah. Just because I'm Prime doesn't mean I'm an asshole. At least I try not to be. What part of 'spoiling you rotten' did I not make clear?"

She sat up and looked at him. "Really? I can have a wedding?"

"We need to set down some ground rules first."

"Ah. Okay. Is this where you become an asshole?"

"Is this where you become Bridezilla?"

She fell back against the bed. "Holy crap." She squealed in protest when he flipped her over and swatted her, hard, across the ass.

"What was that for?" she screamed.

"A warning." He leaned in and kissed her, distracting her. "You're too beautiful to swear like that."

"You are *sooo* not going to spank me on a regular basis, dude."

He fixed his eyes on her and she melted again.

"Oh, really?" he asked.

Unable to speak, she nodded.

"Then you'd better clean up your mouth. I'll give you some time to work on it. I don't care if you swear occasionally, but try to find some more ladylike alternatives."

"You're on thin ice, dude."

"I like swimming in cold water."

She tried for a stony face and couldn't maintain it. She finally laughed. When she did, he smiled.

"Get the tantrums out of your system now, baby. I don't want to be like that with you. I know this is a lot to learn, just let us teach you." He pulled her into his arms. "Let's go over some ground rules. You need to do what we say. Usually we'll give you a say in the matter, but we get the final vote. There's going to be times it doesn't go your way, and you have to accept that."

She frowned. "I'm not a kid."

"Considering we're over two hundred years older than you, uh, yeah, you're a kid."

"Don't you dare pull the 'because I'm older' bullshit."

He frowned. "Mouth."

She stuck her tongue out at him. He tried to frown, but he laughed. "You either like getting spanked or you're in for an eye-opening experience." He sighed. "Most of the time, there won't be an issue. There are going to be times you have to adhere to certain protocols. Like around other Council members, other shifters. And if you don't follow those, we won't hesitate to correct you. In public."

From the stern tone of his voice she knew he was serious.

He continued. "You can't play us against each other, either. We catch you doing that, you're definitely getting spanked. If you ask one of us something and they don't give you an answer you like, you can't come running to someone else and try to get your way."

"But you're in charge!"

"And I stay that way because we have clear communication around here. I would strongly suggest you learn to get all three of us together to talk about stuff that matters. Big stuff. Then the three of us can put our heads together and come to a decision. If you want something and ask only one of us and they say no, that's it."

"That sounds pretty dam—dang petty."

He smiled when he heard her catch herself. "No, it's to preserve order. I'm not going to overrule one of them unless it's something serious, like a violation of the Code. They know the Code as well as I do, so I doubt that's an issue."

"And what exactly is *that*?"

"You'll learn it. We'll teach you. I also suggest you learn to ask questions before jumping to conclusions or getting upset without all the information."

She reddened. "I'm sorry. I pitch a good tantrum."

"So I see. There's no reason for that." He leaned in and kissed her. "Give us a chance to show you how much we love you. I promise, in a few months, you'll understand." He thought for a moment. "We need to get your stuff moved here and discuss what you want to do with your house."

Sadness again. "I really have to quit, huh?"

He nodded. "I'm sorry, sweetheart, but there's too much risk. If you were in a low-profile profession and you worked locally, I would let you keep your job if that's what you wanted. What happens in ten or twenty years when you don't look any older? We have to keep a low profile. Right now, everyone thinks we're the grandsons of the original owners."

"What if I wasn't on the air?"

He studied her. "What do you mean?"

She swallowed hard. She didn't want to give up her job. Being crew was better than nothing. "What if...what if I go back to behind the scenes? One of the producers is going on maternity leave in a couple of weeks. I could volunteer to fill her slot. I wouldn't be on camera."

"You're living *here*. With us. That means two hours a day spent commuting, there and back. That's a lot of driving."

"I know."

He studied her for a long moment. "Do you have any vacation time coming?"

"A week."

"Can you take it this week?"

She melted under the power of his eyes. "I guess."

He leaned in and kissed her nose. "Take the vacation time. Call them today and arrange it." He sighed. "I will *not* give you an answer today about you keeping your job. However, I will think about it and give you my answer at the end of your vacation time. But if you bug me or the others about it before then, I will tell you no. Understand?"

She nodded. "What do I tell my boss about needing vacation?"

"The truth." He stroked her cheek and she closed her eyes, enjoying the feel of his warm flesh against hers. "That you need some personal time."

"Oh fu…dge."

"What?"

"My mom's coming to visit in eight weeks. She's supposed to stay for a month."

"So?"

"What do you mean, so?" She waved her hand at the bedroom. "I guess we can get by on the wedding. How do we explain all of us being in the same bedroom?"

He smirked. "This house has eight bedrooms. Who's to say who sleeps where?"

"Oh." *That was easy.* "And back to the subject of a wedding, how do we exactly do that? Polygamy is illegal in Florida."

"You legally marry me."

"Prime perk."

The corner of his mouth turned up in a smile. "You're getting the hang of it. We'll have a ceremony for Brodey and Cail, too. They'll wear wedding rings. Just because I'll be your husband in legal designation doesn't make them any less your husbands. Getting married is a technicality. It's to legally protect you, make sure you have full rights to our assets, because the only thing that matters to us is what happened last night."

She rubbed her shoulder. "Did you have to bite me so fu…freaking hard?"

"Let me look at it." She turned and he pulled up the T-shirt, ran his fingers over her shoulder. "It's mostly healed already. And it looks beautiful on you. That's proof to others of our kind that you are well and truly taken." He leaned in and feathered his lips over her flesh. She closed her eyes and tried to hold back a moan at how good it felt. Then he kissed her shoulder and dropped her shirt.

"Yeah, you guys well and truly took me last night, all right," she snarked.

He was going to reply when the front door opened and slammed shut. Brodey and Cail crowded through the bedroom door with broad, beaming grins on their faces.

"She's awake!" Cail said. They pushed and shoved and Brodey made it to her first and kissed her, followed by Cail.

"Why aren't you outside?" Ain asked.

"We're done with the morning stuff," Brodey said. "Time for lunch."

"That was record time for you two assholes."

"Hey! How come you get to swear and I don't?" she complained.

Ain leaned in and kissed her, deeply, distracting her. "Because I say so," he said with a smile.

"Argh!"

Cail laughed. "You realize he's teasing, right? He's just a little traditional. He wants you to be more ladylike."

She looked at Ain. When he winked she felt her stomach flutter with desire and her aggravation at him sailed right out the window.

Chapter Nine

The men cooked her a delicious brunch while she called and arranged her time off. After, Cail and Brodey went outside to finish working and Ain carted her back to bed when she tried to argue about going home to get some things.

"You *are* going to rest today." He glared. "That's an order."

Her will melted again. "Fine!" she huffed.

He'd pulled on a pair of shorts. She still wore the T-shirt. He reached for the TV remote and stretched out in bed next to her. "You went through a lot last night." He curled an arm around her. "I want you to rest. You don't have to go today."

"I'm not an invalid."

He nuzzled her forehead. "We know, sweetie. Please, just rest today. Let us have fun spoiling you rotten, okay? We spent a lot of lonely years waiting for you."

That softened her. If she was complaining about a year since her last relationship, she could only imagine…

"Then at least talk to me." She reached for the remote and turned the volume down on the TV. "Tell me about your family."

"We've got ten brothers scattered around the world. Shifters. Another fifteen siblings that have already died. Our parents died over twenty-five years ago in a car crash."

"I'm sorry."

He shrugged. "The old movie fantasy is just that. We can shift whenever we want, although full moons give us extra energy and stamina. We heal much faster than a human, our bodies can take a lot more punishment, but we can still be killed."

"So our kids…" She didn't want to think about that. At least she'd had her Pill for the day. Thank God she kept the packet in her purse.

"I don't have exact numbers, obviously. Most shifters are male, there are few female shifters. Not every child a shifter has is a shifter. Maybe half of them. Some couples never have a child that shifts, some have every child with the right genes."

He rolled to his side and stroked her cheek. "I meant it when I said you're not going to spend your life pregnant. We would like to eventually have kids, but if you decide you don't want any, then that's it."

He laced his fingers through hers and brought her hand to his mouth, kissed it. "I know there's a lot to learn about what we are, and yes, we will have final say on things, but I also meant it when I said that we will devote our lives to making you happy. We have to protect our secret. We have to abide by Clan protocols and the Code of the Ancients." He smiled. "But once all this settles down, you're going to find you've got a lot more power over us than you might think you do right now."

He spent the afternoon answering her questions. It was obvious she was a reporter because he never got a chance to ask her anything.

She was surprised to find when she floated a few trial balloons for wedding ideas that he was agreeable within certain limits. He didn't want a huge crowd of people, fine with her, and the station couldn't film it for obvious reasons. The budget he allowed her was many times what she expected and had ever planned to use in her wildest dreams.

An idea hit her. "How much money are you guys worth?"

"Does it matter?"

"I'm curious."

"Cail does the bookkeeping. Let's just say you don't have any worries."

"Humor me. Give me a ballpark."

He shrugged. "He told me when he did taxes this year our

declared assets were around sixty million. That's not all cash, obviously. We've got real estate, investments. And that's not counting some off-shore accounts and the Swiss bank accounts."

She blinked, trying to absorb that information. When she could finally speak again, she asked, "Then why are you running a cattle ranch?"

He shrugged. "Have to do something. We like it. We like the area, it's easy to stay under the radar. In another fifteen or twenty years we might talk about moving again somewhere else." He rubbed her legs and back for her, both relaxing her and setting off a flurry of delicious sensations in her belly.

She'd pulled the T-shirt off. Seemed pointless to wear it. "I know something else you can do." She playfully wiggled her hips. She was still a little sore although the full-body massage he'd given her had helped.

He gently patted her ass. "Maybe later, sweetheart."

She rolled over and pouted. "I'm okay. Just a little sore."

"Maybe after dinner." He gave her a look she was quickly coming to think of as "the look." "Don't get pushy. We'll have a lot of years together."

Eventually she did fall asleep again. When she awoke alone in bed it was after six o'clock. She pulled on the T-shirt and walked into the kitchen. The men weren't there, but she heard them outside talking. She found a bottle of Tylenol and washed three of them down with water. She'd awoken with another thought that irritated the snot out of her.

Prime or not, Ain was getting a piece of her mind.

The men walked in a few minutes later and smiled when they saw her in the kitchen, until they realized she was upset.

"What's wrong?" Ain asked.

She crossed her arms and refused to look in their eyes or it would totally ruin her stewed mood. "You guys are just assuming I'm going to marry you."

The men exchanged a puzzled look. "But we were discussing what you wanted to do," Ain said.

"And none of you jerks have even asked me to marry you!"

The men looked stunned, then laughed. Ain swept her into his arms before she could protest, with Brodey and Cail flanking them, pressing close, holding her between them. Ain kissed her and she knew, dammit, she *would* melt. She couldn't resist him.

He dropped to one knee and produced a small box from the pocket of his shorts. Inside, a gorgeous sapphire and diamond ring that brought tears to her eyes. "Will you marry me?"

Okay, crazy mood swings, but she had a hunky guy. *Three* hunky guys. She eagerly bobbed her head. "Yes!"

Cail and Brodey each held one of her hands, and they knelt, too. Brodey asked first, "Will you marry me, too?"

She laughed. "Yes."

"Don't forget me," Cail teased. "Will you marry me?"

Okay, they had her, from head to…well, tail. She laughed harder. "Yes, cripes, yes, I'll marry all three of you."

She pulled off her grandmother's rings and transferred them to her right hand. Ain slid the engagement ring onto her left ring finger. "You need to learn patience, sweetheart. We were going to do this after dinner." He stood and kissed her. Then Brodey and Cail each took turns kissing her. By the time Cail released her she wanted them to cart her back to bed and make love to her all night long.

Instead, Ain made her sit on the couch and watch TV while he helped his brothers cook dinner. *At least they're not turning me into a scullery maid*, she thought. *Maybe he really did mean they were going to spoil me rotten.*

After a good dinner, Brodey scooped her into his arms and carried her to the bedroom while Ain and Cail took care of the dishes. "You look beautiful in my shirt, babe."

"Oh, this is yours?" Come to think of it, it did smell like Brodey. She couldn't explain why the men smelled different to her. It was a subtle difference, something very faint, not like a cologne. Ain had a musky scent with almost a hint of something like eucalyptus, masculine. Brodey reminded her of cinnamon and nutmeg. Cail's unique scent conjured thoughts of fresh-cut hay, sweet and earthy.

Brodey gently placed her on the bed and curled up beside her. "Yeah." He kissed her.

Fuck, I'm sooo screwed.

A wave of need washed through her. She wrapped her arms and legs around him and tried to hump his leg.

He pulled the shirt up and gently sucked one of her nipples, drawing a moan from her. "How you feel?" he asked.

"I'm not swinging off a chandelier tonight, but don't leave me hanging."

He quickly stripped, then kissed her belly as he moved lower. "No, sweetie, I won't do that. Never again." He settled his mouth over her mound. That's where he was when Cail and Ain walked in.

"Told you," Cail said as he stripped off his shirt. "You owe me five bucks. Knew he couldn't keep his hands off her."

Ain didn't respond, just rolled his eyes and started stripping.

Elain didn't care because she was in heaven. Brodey had her squirming on the bed. When Cail pressed his lips to hers she grabbed him and fucked her tongue deep into his mouth, drawing an amused laugh. He managed to come up for air.

"I'd say she's in the mood to play."

Brodey clamped his hands around her thighs and drove his tongue into her sex. Ain stretched out on her other side and turned her face to his.

"Look at me," he whispered.

She forced her eyes open.

"We love you. We promise we'll take care of you, baby. We'll spend our lives making you happy, I swear it, we all do. Just trust us that we know what we're talking about."

She nodded.

He kissed her, and then Brodey did something delicious between her legs that set off a mind-blowing climax. She cried out as Ain whispered encouragement to her while she trembled on the bed between them.

Just when she approached the point she didn't think she could take it anymore, Brodey relented and lifted his mouth and replaced it with his stiff cock.

They both moaned as he thrust home. He pulled her into his lap and she wrapped her legs and arms around him. He pressed his lips to her ear. "I love you, sweetie. Jesus, I love you so much."

She shivered in his arms. She felt it from him. It wasn't just bullshit words from her men.

Her men.

He stroked her back as he rolled his hips beneath her. She pressed her lips to his shoulder when a persistent thought kept bumping against her mind.

She bit him.

He yelped, but his thrusts deepened, quickened, and she held on for the ride as he came. Then he gently lowered her to the mattress. "Holy fuck, that was great, babe! You okay?"

She nodded. She was still a little achy but she wouldn't let it interfere with her fun. "You okay?" She traced her fingers across the mark she'd left. Not hard enough to break the skin, but apparently enough to flip his switch.

Saying she'd kill for his broad, beaming grin wasn't an exaggeration. He nuzzled her nose with his, tenderly kissed her. "That was perfect," he whispered. "You're perfect. It's like you read my mind."

She looked at Cail and crooked a finger at him.

He grinned and rolled on top of her. "Yeeeessss?"

Kissing him in reply, he slipped inside her and slowly stroked, a different style than the night before. As she sensed him rolling toward his orgasm, she had a thought and raked her nails down his back before digging them into his ass.

"Do it," she said, "Come for me, baby."

He let out a loud cry and buried his cock even deeper, held still, his eyes closed.

She wouldn't let him go, held him with his face resting on her shoulder. When he finally recovered he looked at her. "That was amazing!"

"It's what you wanted, right?"

He smiled and nuzzled her nose. "Yeah."

Ain grinned. "That's fantastic! Usually it takes weeks for that to start happening."

She shot him an annoyed glare. "Uh, what about last night?"

"I told you, the ceremony's different. Usually it takes a while for it to kick in full-time after that."

Cail kissed her and carefully rolled off her. That left Ain. She climbed on top of him and kissed him. "Your turn."

He smiled. "I wasn't going to say anything in case you were too sore."

"Don't expect anything else out of me tonight. Just enjoy yourself."

He did. She wouldn't deny feeling their thick cocks inside her was amazing. He rested his hands on her hips and thrust up into her. She stroked his chest. All three men were lightly fuzzed with fine, dark down, thank God they weren't frickin' furry.

He met her gaze and she felt it, his thought.

I love you.

She smiled and thought back, *I love you, too.*

He grinned. Then he grabbed her hips and finished in three strokes.

Cail and Brodey knew something had happened.

"What?" Brodey asked. "What is it?"

She looked at him. *I love your purple eyes.*

He looked confused. "What? Babe, my eyes aren't…" Realization dawned and he grinned. "So that *is* how you knew. Aw, fuck me!"

"Already did, sweetie." *I love you.*

He laughed, leaned in and kissed her. *I love you, too.*

She turned to Cail. "Can you guys hear when I do that with one of the others?"

He shook his head. "I know you're talking, but it's like hearing it through a wall. It's not clear."

She met his eyes. *I love you.*

His broad, beaming smile and sweet brown eyes melted her. *Honey, you have no idea how much I love you.*

Ain grabbed her and gently pulled her down to the bed, into his arms. "Bed time. You can experiment with your new superpowers tomorrow."

She laughed. "Superpowers?"

He kissed the back of her neck. "Yeah."

Apparently Cail got to cuddle up on her other side that night. She suspected one of Ain's Prime perks was getting to be by her side every night and that the other two would have to trade off.

All things considered, she thought she was handling this fairly well. Shape-shifters real, check. Hunky triplet love muffins who only had eyes for her, check.

Not just hunky…

"Hey, Brodey," she mumbled.

"What, babe?"

"Speak Scottish for me."

He laughed from somewhere on the other side of Cail. "Frrrreeedooom!"

Ain and Cail groaned. "Don't get him started!" they said together.

She smiled and closed her eyes and drifted to sleep in the arms of her men.

THE END

Storm Warning

Triple Trouble 2

Tymber Dalton

Siren Publishing

Ménage Amour

STORM WARNING

Triple Trouble 2

TYMBER DALTON
Copyright © 2009

Chapter One

Elain lay on her stomach on a towel by the pool, trying to relax in the sun. When the huge, black, green-eyed wolf crept out of the nearby woods, it soundlessly leapt over the fence surrounding the pool and stalked her.

Moving silently, it circled around her until it pounced and started frantically humping the back of her leg.

"I don't give a crap how much I love you," she mumbled, not moving, not even opening her eyes. "If you want to fuck me, Brodey, you damn well better shift back. You try to make me do it like this, I'll dope your dinner and shave you bald. You'll look like a freaking mutant Chihuahua next time you shift."

The wolf changed into a naked man, who stretched over her. He laughed and kissed her between her shoulder blades. "Would you really do that to me, baby doll?"

"You know I would. Ain and Cail would help me."

"You're probably right." He made her roll onto her side and kissed her. Wolf or dog, he was still fricking hard. "Is this better?"

"Much better, furball."

"How did you know it was me?"

She wrapped her arms around him. "I heard you." The middle

brother of the Lyall triplets had gorgeous green eyes that always melted her.

Who was she kidding? All three brothers could turn her insides into melted marshmallows, whether Beta Brodey's green eyes, Gamma Cailean's sweet brown gaze, or Prime Alpha Aindreas' piercing grey intensity.

"I didn't make any noise!"

"Your mental drooling. I heard you before you ever left the woods by that pond. You kept thinking, 'Jesus, I'm so fucking horny,' all the way over the fence. Practically screaming it by the time you got to me. I'd have to be deaf not to hear that."

He sat up. "No shit? Really? You heard me that far away? By the pond?"

She nodded. "Yeah. Why?"

Apparently this news was enough to distract him. His stiff cock softened as he looked contemplative. "I mean, that's totally unusual."

"Well, according to Ain I'm screwing up the high end of the bell curve by already hearing you guys in my brain this soon to begin with." She'd only been with the brothers for four days. It was still difficult for her to think of herself as their "mate."

"No, honey, you don't understand. Normally a mate can only pick up thoughts at a really close distance."

"You were close."

"As in the same room. Sometimes, only within feet. Not a quarter mile away or more. That's where the pond is."

"No shi—shinola?"

He grinned and nuzzled her nose. "I won't tell Ain if you swear. It doesn't bother me like it bothers him."

"I thought you had to abide by the Prime's edicts?" she groused. Elain still struggled to learn all the ins and outs of being a mate to the triplet shape-shifter brothers. All three men were Alphas. When Prime Alpha Ain set down an edict, the others, and now Elain as well, were compelled to abide by it.

"He didn't issue an edict about you swearing. He just told you he wanted you to clean up your mouth." He laughed and grabbed her hand, stood, and pulled her to her feet. "Come on."

"Where are we going?"

"We need to tell Cail. This is incredible."

Even more incredible was that she could still walk after the recent events. Less than two weeks ago, she'd let a large black wolf-like dog with gorgeous green eyes ride back to the TV station with her and her cameraman after it had jumped into their van at the First Annual Arcadia Highland Games. When two days later she reunited him, Brodey, as it turned out to be, with his "owner" Aindreas Lyall, she had no idea that the three hunkalicious brothers had instinctively picked her as their mate, their "One."

That first meeting with Aindreas, Elain thought he came across as a standoffish jerk even though the other two brothers seemed like sweetheart cuties. When Brodey and Cailean showed up out of the blue at the station a few days later to take her to lunch, it had ended in a quick tryst in the parking lot that left her, well, perpetually horny.

That had led to them inviting her to dinner a few days later at their cattle ranch in Arcadia, an invitation she couldn't refuse. Hours later, her world had rolled over one hundred and eighty degrees on its axis. Shape-shifters were real, and she'd essentially married the three brothers, who happened to be over two hundred and thirty years old. Despite looking maybe thirty, their jet black hair was untouched by grey. Also not a bad deal considering they were rich and hunky.

And they only had eyes for her.

They found Cail in the study where he did paperwork and bookkeeping for the ranch operations. Brodey wrapped his arms around Elain and nibbled on the back of her neck.

She argued with her knees to keep them supporting her. Dammit, the men seemed to know exactly what buttons to push to melt her body into a puddle.

"Guess what, Cail," Brodey said.

He didn't look up from his computer. "You're horny."

Elain laughed. "Guess what else?"

He finally sat back and turned, smiled at her. "What?"

Brodey explained. Cail frowned, looked contemplative. Even though only minutes younger than his two brothers, he had a more thoughtful nature. "That's...unheard of."

Brodey nodded. "I know! Isn't it great?"

Cail caught her hand and gently pulled her from Brodey's arms and into his lap. She wore a one-piece bathing suit she suspected wouldn't stay on her long. "It's not bad. It's just...weird."

"Gee, thanks, Cail," she snarked.

He kissed her. "You're not weird, babe. I mean I've never heard of a non-shifter mate able to pick up thoughts that far away." He stroked her thigh as he stared at Brodey. "We should call Ain and tell him." Aindreas was supervising the daily activities on the other side of the ranch where the business end of things took place. Just because the brothers now had their One didn't mean they could slough off their daily duties.

"He'll be back soon enough," Brodey said. "No reason to bug him, I left him in the northwest pasture. He'll just get pissed he has to go back out later." Brodey tried to pull her from Cail's lap but he held on.

"Ahem, boys? I'm not a doggy tug toy."

"I wanted to play with her," Brodey whined.

"Oh, Goddess, you fucking baby," Cail scolded. "You got to spend a couple of nights alone with her that me and Ain didn't."

"Yeah, and I was shifted the whole time, too. It's not like I got to have fun with her. No offense, babe." He still held her hand. His cock had started inflating again. "C'mon, Cail. Give her back."

She pulled her hand free and stood up. "All right, stop it. Both of you." She tried to stay irritated and couldn't. The sweet look on their faces melted her reserves.

Elain made a big show of rolling her eyes and dramatically

sighing. She walked toward their shared bedroom. "All right. If you boys absolutely, positively can't wait—"

The men raced past her, beating her to the bedroom. Cail was naked by the time he landed on the bed next to Brodey.

She laughed. At least she felt wanted, no denying that.

As predicted, the men quickly rid her of her bathing suit, not that she minded. Cail kissed her while Brodey dove between her legs. She sighed, content, as he eagerly laved her clit with his tongue. This part of their unusual relationship had, surprisingly enough, been the easiest to wrap her mind around. The boys had already proposed to her even though she would legally marry only Ain.

Spending an extended life in the arms of these three men wouldn't be a sacrifice, that's for damn sure.

Cail broke their kiss and dropped his head to her breast, teasing one nipple with his tongue while his fingers tweaked the other. She wrapped her fingers in his hair as she let out a hungry moan. Brodey gripped her thighs with his large hands and fucked his tongue inside her before slowly dragging it across her clit. Then he switched to feather-light flicks with his tongue that soon had her shuddering and crying out as she came.

She'd had more sex in the past few days than she'd had in the past few years. Best sex of her life, too.

"That's what I wanted to hear," Brodey said with a chuckle as he kissed his way up her body. Cail sat up and held her as Brodey lifted her feet to his shoulder.

Elain smiled. "Going back to work will be a vacation from having my legs in the air," she joked.

A brief frown flitted across his face before he slowly stroked his stiff cock inside her. "You think so, huh?"

She loved the feel of any of them inside her. "Yeah."

As horny as Brodey was, he didn't last long. She turned in Cail's arms and kissed him, stroked his cock. "What about you?"

He smiled. "What about me?"

She gently squeezed his cock. "Anything you want taken care of?"

He laughed. "What did you have in mind?"

Elain grinned and bent her head to his lap and enjoyed the feel of his hands fisting in her hair as she sucked his cock deep into her mouth.

Brodey moaned. "Jesus, that's gorgeous!"

"Shut up," Cail growled. "You had your turn."

Elain tried not to laugh but couldn't help it. She sat up despite Cail's disappointed moan. "You two are too much." When Ain wasn't around, the two "younger" brothers frequently bickered.

She pushed Cail down onto the bed and straddled his stiff shaft, taunted him. "What do you want, baby?"

He gripped her hips and thrust into her. "That, you little tease."

Brodey knelt behind her, his hand finding her clit and stroking it. She relaxed against him as Cail slowly thrust. Yes, this was a gooooood life.

Cail reached up and played with her nipples, triggering her spiral into another climax. When he felt her muscles gripping his cock, he grabbed her hips again and thrust hard, trying to finish with her. She threw her head back against Brodey's shoulder, trusting him to hold on to her as she trembled and cried out in his arms.

A moment later she slumped to the bed, the two men cradling her between them. She was draped over Cail's chest while Brodey tightly curled against her back. And that's where they still lay nearly an hour later, dozing, when Ain walked into the bedroom.

"I should have known."

"Busted," Brodey muttered against the back of her neck.

"It's your fault, Brod," Cail mumbled from Elain's other side.

Ain's deep laughter prompted Elain to open her eyes. Dressed in jeans and a work shirt, he leaned against the doorway. Damn, he looked yummy. "There's plenty of room," she said.

He walked over to the bed and leaned in to kiss her. "One of us has to work for a living around here, since my two lazy brothers seem to have forgotten we've got a ranch to run."

"Fuck you—" Brodey didn't get the rest of the sentence out, because Ain rolled him off the bed onto the floor.

"You were saying?" Ain asked, his voice low and growly.

Brodey sat up and glared at him over the bed, but didn't respond. Elain noticed the hard look in Ain's eyes, the steely set to his jaw, until Brodey looked away. "I'll get dressed."

"Don't bother, I need help cutting cattle. You might as well shift now. Truck's outside."

Brodey stood and leaned in to give Elain one last kiss. "See you later, babe." He shifted and trotted out of the bedroom.

Cail sat up and ran a hand through his hair. "I need to get back to my paperwork." He pulled her to him and kissed her. "Oh, Ain, listen to this." He gave his older brother a quick run-down of what Brodey had discovered.

Ain brushed a stray hair from her forehead and tucked it behind her ear. "Really?"

Elain nodded.

"What do you think it means?" Ain asked Cail.

Elain had also noticed that while Ain was Prime Alpha, he didn't hesitate to ask Cail's opinion on things. Brodey was more brawn than brain, even if he did have moments of brilliance.

Cail shrugged. "I don't know. We should experiment, see how far away she can hear and send."

"Good idea. Why don't you guys do that this afternoon while I keep the horn dog distracted." Ain winked at Elain and leaned in for another kiss. She wanted to rip his clothes off him but knew he was more in a work mindset.

"Okay," Cail said.

Chapter Two

Instead of a shower, Cail and Elain jumped into the pool for a couple of minutes before getting dressed and grabbing a work truck. He drove them out to one of the remote pastures, away from roads and people, so they could have privacy. The three thousand-acre ranch provided a lot of that.

"We need to work with you on fine-tuning your ability since it's so strong," Cail said.

"Then why did we come out here?"

"What am I thinking?"

She shrugged. "I don't know."

"Try to listen for my thoughts."

She frowned and studied him, trying to concentrate. "I don't hear anything."

"Okay. What about now?" He mentally spoke to her. *"Can you hear me now? ...Good."*

She laughed. "Yes, I heard you."

Cail looked thoughtful. "You need us to actively think to you. Brodey must have been doing it subconsciously."

"He was horny, kept saying it over and over."

Cail laughed. "That figures."

"Again, why are we out here?"

They were alone in the remote pasture. He stripped. When he peeled off his jeans—she loved that they frequently went commando—she wanted to jump him again despite their earlier encounter.

He grinned and folded his clothes, laid them in the back of the truck. "I heard that, honey."

She blushed. "Can't blame me for wanting it."

He leaned in and kissed her, then shifted into a huge, black wolf-like dog with big brown eyes. *"Can you hear me now?"* he thought to her.

"Yeah, I hear you."

"I'm going to run. Yell at me when you can't hear me anymore. I want to see the distance."

"Okay."

He took off, singing *Cheeseburger in Paradise* as he ran.

Elain laughed.

She could still hear him when he disappeared into the woods over one hundred yards away. He gradually faded out. When she couldn't hear him anymore she screamed, "Now! I can't hear you!"

He faded back in.

"Yes!"

"Fuck. That's…incredible."

"What?"

"Don't scream now, babe. Think to me."

She wasn't sure how to project. She closed her eyes. *"Can you hear me like this?"*

"Yeah." His mental voice sounded amazed. *"You sing something to me like that. I want to see if your reach to me is greater than mine to you."*

"What do you want me to sing?"

"Whatever you want."

Figures, put on the spot, she couldn't remember the words to anything.

"Hum something in your head. Anything."

She finally remembered the words for *Come Monday.*

He laughed. *"I'm so glad you like Buffett, babe. Keep singing until I tell you to stop."*

She did, making it through the whole song and then starting over again. She'd made it nearly halfway through her second repetition when he stopped her.

"Okay, babe. Wow."

"What?"

"I'll be right back."

She watched as a few moments later he broke through the woods and crossed the pasture at a full run. With his body stretched long and low to the ground, his legs took huge strides that set her heart thumping in response. She didn't want to do the deed with them while they were shifted, but knowing there was a hunky man inside that animal...

She sighed.

All mine.

He slowed as he approached her, then trotted up and jumped into the truck bed. He cocked his head at her.

"What?" she asked out loud.

He looked around, shifted back, and then crooked his finger at her.

She nervously glanced around, but when she spotted his stiff cock she scrambled up into the truck bed next to him.

"So you think I look sexy when I run, huh?" He pulled her down on top of him and kissed her.

"Yeah."

He lifted her shirt and bra and latched onto her right breast with his mouth, rolled her left nipple with his fingers. After a few minutes of this her panties were soaked through. She ground her hips against him, his erection pressing against her through her shorts.

"Please!"

"Please what?" he growled against her flesh.

"Don't tease me."

He rolled over and yanked her shorts down and off her. "You mean you want my cock inside you?"

Another flood of moisture to her already soaked sex. "Yes!"

He didn't bother taking her shirt off. He grabbed her hips and sank his full length into her with a satisfied moan. "Jesus, you feel sooo good, babe."

He slowly stroked, stretching his body against hers so his cock glided along her clit as he thrust. Cail had a special touch his brothers didn't have in this way. He was able to get her over the edge just from fucking her without any other assistance.

She ground her lips against him. "I'm going to need a shower when we get back to the house," she gasped.

He grinned. "How about I toss you into the pool?"

"Great. Brodey will be humping me before I even get out." Ain was the strong, brooding brother. Cail was sensitive and thoughtful.

Brodey...

Well, Brodey was a big, playful, perpetually horny puppy.

He laughed. "Probably."

She closed her eyes, working her hips with his as he found the perfect speed and angle. Elain raked her fingers down his back, which drew a satisfied hiss from Cail.

"That's it...you know what I like," he whispered.

Her own release close, she dug her nails into his ass and his resulting moan helped her clear the crest. As he felt her coming he thrust, hard, nearly driving her into the truck cab with the force. They moaned and writhed together as they came until Cail finally collapsed, spent, on top of her.

"Dammit, babe," he whispered, "you're amazing."

He helped her put herself back together and grabbed his own clothes. She had to admit she enjoyed having all this land to get nekkid on without worrying about someone seeing them. If she kept this up, she'd end up bow-legged.

Not that she minded in the least.

She cuddled close to his side for the ride back to the house. Why bother with a bathing suit? She dropped her clothes on the edge of the pool and dove into the cool water. A few moments later she heard a splash in the water behind her. Before she could turn, Brodey had grabbed her and spun her around, a huge grin on his face.

She wrapped her arms and legs around him and gasped as his cock slid home.

"Well, hello to you too, buddy."

His hands cupped her ass. "You know damn well if you swim naked around me I can't resist."

She laughed. "You weren't around when I jumped in."

"I heard you and Cail return. I was out in the equipment barn."

"Ah. Again, you weren't around when I jumped in."

He kissed her and they sank below the water. When they re-emerged a moment later he'd maneuvered them toward the shallow end of the pool so his feet touched.

Playful puppy—that more than accurately described Beta brother Brodey.

He certainly loved to splash around in the pool with her.

"You should shift into a Portuguese Water Dog instead of a wolf," she quipped.

"Ain beat you to that one by about twenty years."

"Damn."

He kissed her, thrusting into her. Then he dropped his head to her shoulder. "You gonna come for me, baby?" he gasped.

She held him close and stroked his hair. "No, sweetie. You have some fun. You guys have worn me out today."

She didn't have to ask twice. She held on for the ride as his large cock frantically pounded into her, not nearly as hard a fucking as it would have felt like if he had her flat on her back in bed. She suspected it was one of the reasons he loved tagging her in the water.

Elain nuzzled his ear, then bit down, hard.

He yelped, but with a final thrust he cried out as he came, holding her tightly against him.

"Fuck!" he whispered, still trembling.

"You like that?"

He laughed, then raised his head to look at her. "Hell, yeah. You know I did." He kissed her. "You heard me thinking loud again, huh?"

Cail loved it when she got a little rough with her nails. Brodey enjoyed a little nip and tickle. Ain was more on the traditional side.

"You think pretty damn loud when you're horny, sweetie."

He peeled her off him, holding her in his arms as he carried her out of the pool. "I can't help it. That's what you do to me."

She didn't doubt him or the other two men. She'd never believed in love at first sight—or bite, in Brodey's case—but whatever magic she had with these three men, she wouldn't deny it felt real and strong.

* * * *

Over dinner, Brodey and Ain were amazed to hear Cail's report. "That's incredible!" Ain said.

Cail nodded. "You're telling me. I couldn't believe it."

Elain looked at the men. "Yeah, but that's good, right?"

Brodey shrugged. "It's not good or bad, babe. It just is." He stood and carried his empty plate to the sink. "Oh, do you want me to run you back over to Venice to get more of your stuff tomorrow?" He'd already drove her there once so she could pack a few days worth of clothes.

Elain was dying to ask Ain if he'd made up his mind about letting her go back to work or not. He'd told her he'd think about it, and then give her his answer at the end of the vacation days she'd taken to spend with them. He'd warned her if she bugged him about it he would automatically say no.

She understood why they didn't want her to work on-air, but she hoped he'd agree to let her take over a producer job behind the scenes. The station manager had already agreed to go along with it, even though he was a little puzzled at her eagerness to ditch the on-air job she'd worked so hard to land.

"Let's hold off a few days, Brodey. I'm okay for now. I need to go grocery shopping tomorrow anyway. I'm going to cook you guys a nice dinner tomorrow night. You've been spoiling me rotten." She started to stand to take her plate to the sink. Cail beat her to it. She had to admit the men treated her like a princess. She kissed him before he walked away with her dishes.

"Spoiling you rotten is our job," Ain said with a playful smile. "Better get used to it."

* * * *

Later that evening, Ain got on the phone to one of his distant cousins. Jocko Connelly still lived at a Clan compound up in Maine. He also knew a lot of arcane and virtually useless information about lineage and other Clans in addition to his wealth of practical shape-shifter knowledge.

"Hey! Aindreas!" Jocko still spoke with a Scottish brogue. "How ye be? Haven't heard from ye in a long time. Congratulations are in order, so the rumor mill flows."

"Doing good, and yes, thank you. Have a question for you."

"Anything. Shoot."

"Out of curiosity, what might be involved that gives a non-shifter mate the ability to hear her mates' thoughts a long distance away? Over a quarter mile away when she tunes in and deliberately pays attention. And…to project that far."

There was a brief moment of stunned silence. "Really? Ye dunt seh?"

"Do you think it's because we're triplet Alphas?"

"I dunno, boyo. Could be, could be. You're the only triplets, ye know that. And you're all Alphas. There's stuff that might apply to ye that applies to no one else."

That's no help. "Any other ideas?"

"Well, I've heard of cases where half-shifter mates had that kind of ability, but I take it she's not?"

Ain thought about it. "No. She would know if she was, right?"

"Well, you'd think, laddie. I mean, that's not the kind of family secret that gets held back in our kind."

"She was totally shocked to find out what we were. I'd say that's a pretty safe no."

"Eh, well, maybe she's got distant shifter line in her background. That's always a possibility. What's her name?"

"Elain Pardie."

"Hmm. Pardie...Pardie...That sounds familiar. Where's she from?"

Ain felt a pang of guilt that he still didn't know. "I think she grew up in Tampa."

"Let me think on that a while, do some digging. I'll get back to ye."

"Thanks."

Ain tried to shove away the feeling of disquiet in his gut. Elain couldn't be half-shifter, she'd know it. Besides, there's no way her Clan would let her come of age, much less mate, without telling her what she was first.

That couldn't be the answer.

Most of the Clans, including their own, didn't care who their members mated with. Except for the trouble-making Abernathy Clan. They tightly held on to their Alpha shifters and carefully controlled who they met after they came of age until they pinged on a mate. If they didn't ping on one of their own Clan, the mating and marking had to be approved before it could take place, usually with a large dowry involved.

The Abernathies were, if nothing else, efficiently greedy bastards.

Only Alpha shifters had to mate with their One. Problem was, most of the new Abernathy shifters weren't Alphas because their bloodlines had become too inbred. Any shifter not an Alpha could mate to anyone.

Well if they were an Abernathy, to anyone approved of by the Abernathy Clan hierarchy. Abernathies didn't care about people who weren't shifters. For shifters and half-shifters, those matings always had to be pre-approved. Frequently, non-Alpha matings were pre-arranged, even before birth, or so rumors said. To mate outside the Abernathy Clan—or to dare mate inside theirs—without their prior approval would drive them to violence.

Creepy assholes. No wonder that Clan was dying off, thank the Goddess. Ain had even heard stories of Abernathy shifters mating with someone that wasn't approved of by the Abernathy Clan, and the Clan murdered the mate.

Chapter Three

Ain kissed Elain before he untangled himself from her the next morning.

"Where are you going?" she mumbled sleepily.

"I'm sorry, sweetie. You sleep in. I need to help the guys cut cattle this morning." He stroked her back, rubbed her shoulders.

She moaned as she melted into the mattress. "Okay," she mumbled.

He kissed the back of her neck. "Don't worry about fixing us lunch. We've got to run into town for supplies anyway."

"Mmm hmm."

He left, softly closing the bedroom door behind him.

She heard them talking out in the kitchen, smelled coffee and heard Brodey rummaging through a cabinet.

"Fuck," Brodey grumbled.

"What?" That was Cail. She knew his slightly softer tone. Sometimes he still rolled his R's a little, left over from his childhood and years spent living in Scotland.

"We're out of Cheerios!" Brodey whined.

A weary sigh. Definitely Ain. "Just eat something."

"I like Cheerios. You know that. Today's my day for Cheerios. Yesterday was Life, tomorrow is Frosted Mini Wheats."

"Eat something!" Ain growled.

She stifled an amused snort and slowly climbed out of bed. She felt a little sore, comfortably achy. She'd make poor Brodey breakfast so he could quit complaining.

She reached for a T-shirt—Cail's, from the smell of it—and

started for the bedroom door. It finally struck her that she could actually hear the boys as if they were in the same room and not halfway across the house. Normally she wouldn't be able to hear them like this. And to add in the new super-sniffer was pretty amazing.

Wow, Ain wasn't kidding when he said my senses might improve!

She reached for the bedroom doorknob when she heard Brodey speak.

* * * *

"You're really thinking about letting her keep her job?" Brodey asked Ain.

He shook his head. "No. Are you crazy? I know by the end of her vacation time she won't want to go back to work. This way, at least, she'll think she made the decision. It saves me from having to put my foot down."

Cail frowned. "That's a fucking low thing to do, Ain. She loves her job."

Ain slammed his bowl against the counter a little harder than he meant. Fortunately, he didn't break it. "You know as well as I do she can't work now. Especially not at a TV station. Are you crazy?"

Brodey glared. "You shouldn't fuck with her mind like that. Personally, I think you should let her work."

"What? Again, I ask, are you as crazy as Cail?"

Brodey shrugged. "I don't like you messing with her."

"I didn't mess with her. I told her I'd think about it."

"Yeah," Cail said, "but you didn't tell her you'd already made up your mind. That's wrong."

Ain glared at them. "You two don't get to decide this. I do."

"We should get a say in this!" Cail protested. "Do I want her working? Honestly? No. But I want it to be her decision, not some fucking trick. I think that's wrong."

Brodey stood shoulder to shoulder with Cail on this. "You said we weren't going to force her to be our mate. I don't think we should force her to quit her job, either. Yeah, not work on air, okay, I can agree with that. She should get to work if she wants to."

"Her place is here, with us," Ain growled, dropping his voice. "She's our mate. It's our job to provide for her, to take care of her, to keep her happy. That's what we're going to do." He dumped the rest of his cereal, his appetite now gone. "You know damn well she won't want to work after she spends a few more days with us."

Brodey wasn't letting it drop. "I know she can't stay on the air. Let her get a job in town somewhere at least."

Cail nervously looked between the two. "I gotta agree with Brodey on this one, Ain. I don't think it's right to mess with her head."

"Don't push me on this, guys. You know I'm right. Maybe in a few months she can get a job somewhere around Arcadia, close to home, but she can't work at the station. In a few days, she won't want to go back to work anyway. Then she'll think it's her idea and we won't have to fight with her about it. Everyone'll be happy. I'm trying to make this easy on all of us." He angrily stormed out of the kitchen and slammed the back door behind him.

Cail and Brodey exchanged disgusted looks before they followed him out the door.

* * * *

Elain stood by the doorway and listened, her heart in her feet.

Funny, she always thought that was just a stupid metaphor, not a literal sensation.

She trusted Ain. Trusted him! She knew he might not go along with her plan, but she thought he would at least give her the benefit of the doubt and legitimately consider it.

Not at all.

His betrayal hurt. Hurt like hell. A physical ache in her chest.

Funny, she always thought that was a stupid myth, too.

When the men walked out the back door to go to the other side of the property, Elain instinctively acted. Grabbing her overnight bag, she shoved as much as she could fit in it, more than half of what she'd brought over from her house. Ain insisted she take "personal time" from work? By God, she'd use it her way, *not* his.

She got dressed and grabbed her cell phone, charger, purse and keys. The ache in her chest grew heavier, like pressure.

Great. Maybe I'll have a heart attack. That'll show them.

No, not them.

Him. Ain. Brodey and Cail at least sounded as upset as she felt over Ain's revelation.

She stopped at the front door and looked at her ring. How could she marry Ain now? Not when he so obviously didn't respect her. When he wasn't honest with her. When he played mind games with her.

It almost physically hurt slipping the ring off her finger, knowing she would be walking away not only from Ain, but from Brodey and Cail, too. She stepped into the kitchen and set the ring in the middle of the table. She wondered who would find it first and then decided that hurt too much to think about.

Elain threw her things in her car and drove off without looking in the rear view mirror.

* * * *

Elain had made it almost to Arcadia when she thought to turn off her phone. She couldn't answer it. If she did when Ain called, she knew he'd issue one of his "edicts" and she'd turn around without question. As it was, the only way she could bypass his edict about her living at the ranch was because she rationalized she only needed to be home a few minutes. Just long enough to pack a suitcase and book a flight to Spokane to go for a visit. When she thought that, a little of the pressure on her chest eased.

Cail wasn't the only one who could think of loopholes, that's for damn sure.

Fuck Ain.

She didn't even bother trying not to swear. *Fuck him. FUCK him!*

All the way back to Venice, Elain nervously glanced in her rear view mirror. She wasn't sure how much time she'd have before they came looking for her. Only Brodey knew where her house was, but it wouldn't take long for Ain to edict it out of him. By the time she pulled into her driveway, her hands shook from stress.

She quickly ran inside, booted up her computer and repacked. By the time she was ready and had her bags loaded, the computer waited. She quickly found the first flight out of Tampa International for Spokane, leaving in three hours, and booked it. She didn't dare turn on her cell yet.

But she also didn't want Brodey and Cail worried about her, thinking something horrible had happened.

Thinking fast, she composed an email message to Cail's account.

I heard Ain talking to you guys about my job. I also heard you two disagree with him, and I really appreciate it. I'm sorry Cail, Brodey, but no matter how much I love you two, I don't trust that son of a bitch now. I can't risk having contact with Ain and then him issue one of his bullshit edicts to force me back. I need to get away for a while. Please don't worry. Maybe at some point I can talk to you two, but I can't talk to him. I'm sorry. Maybe you can find someone else who won't mind Ain bossing her around without any thoughts to her free will or what she wants or how unhappy she is. I give you guys permission to find someone else or move on or break the whatever you need to let me go. It's okay. I have a feeling I'm going to be miserable without the three of you, but I know I would be more miserable under Ain's thumb if I stayed.

She realized she was crying again.

She hit send, shut the computer down, and then locked the door behind her as she left.

* * * *

When the men returned from the barns and walked in the back door a little after five, Ain immediately went in to take a shower.

Cail looked around. "Where's Elain?"

Brodey shook his head, glanced out a front window. "Car's gone. Probably at the store. Remember, she mentioned that last night."

Cail nodded. "Probably right. She said she wanted to cook a nice dinner for us." He went to his study to check his email.

Brodey headed to the kitchen. He was a little hungry but didn't want to spoil his appetite for dinner.

Snack or not…snack or not…

He opted for a glass of juice. That would help. He poured himself a large glass and settled at the table to finish reading the paper.

Then something in the middle of the table caught his eye.

* * * *

Cail scanned his email and nearly missed the one from Elain. When he opened it, it felt like his heart curled into a tight ball. He had to re-read it several times for it to sink in. She'd sent it before noon.

"Brodey!" His brother didn't respond but maybe it was because he knew his voice sounded weak with shock. "Brod!"

After a long moment, he appeared in the study doorway. "She's gone," Brodey whispered.

Cail turned, startled. "But how did—" He saw the ring in Brodey's hand.

Brodey looked close to tears. "Did she leave a note?"

Cail nodded and stepped away from the computer.

Brodey read her message, his tears openly falling, his jaw clenched in anger. "Fucking bastard! We warned him not to fuck with her like that. Goddammit!"

He shoved the ring into his pocket and disappeared into their bedroom for a moment. Ain was still in the shower. When Brodey reappeared barely a minute later, he had an overnight bag slung over his shoulder. Cail grabbed his arm. "Where are you going?"

"Give me your phone." He pulled his out of his jeans and set it to silent mode, handed it to Cail.

"What?"

"Give me your fucking phone!" Cail handed it over. "I'm going after her. I can't have Assholio in there calling me and ordering me back. Your phone looks like mine. That'll buy me a few hours until I can get a disposable one." He walked toward the front door.

"I'm coming with you!"

Brodey wheeled on him. "No, you're going to fucking stay here and try to keep King Asshole off my tail for a few hours."

"What the fuck am I supposed to tell him?"

"Nothing yet. Pretend you didn't find that email. It'll take me at least an hour to drive to Venice. I bet she's not there, it's been hours since she sent that." Brodey lowered his voice. "I'll try to figure out where she's heading. He's going to edict you into telling him what you know. I won't be able to tell you what I know because of that. Once he edicts you, text me on this phone and tell me it's not safe to call. Okay?"

Cail nodded. "Okay," he softly said.

Brodey started to walk out the door when Cail grabbed him again. "Please tell her I love her, too, when you find her. Okay? And tell her I'm sorry."

He nodded and hugged his brother hard. "I will. You know damn well I will."

Cail watched him drive off. He heard the shower shut off in the master bath and hurried back to his study.

He took down his email and looked at Brodey's phone, set it to total silent, not just vibrate, then put it in his pocket.

He prayed to the Goddess that Brodey could find her.

* * * *

Please, babe, please don't leave us, Brodey silently chanted all the way to Venice. He knew he risked getting a ticket because he pushed the speed limit. When he reached her house his heart sank when he saw her empty driveway.

He pulled in and thought for a moment. How to get in? Then he remembered when he stayed with her while he was shifted, she'd walked him one night and accidentally locked them out.

Spare key.

Still there. He let himself in and immediately walked to her bedroom. She'd left some clothes scattered on the bed, clothes that hadn't been there the other day when he brought her home to pick up some things. Some of the clothes he knew damn well she'd brought over to the house with her. He closed his eyes and smelled the scent of home, the ranch.

Dammit.

He turned on her computer and started searching her desk, found her address book. *Where the hell would she go?* He shoved it into his overnight bag and looked at her browser history.

Ah ha!

Airline tickets.

He opened her email and sure enough, he found an electronic receipt for her ticket with a duplicate of her boarding pass.

Spokane. Who the fuck lived there?

He jumped into her shower, forced himself to hurry despite his impending exhaustion, and changed clothes. Then he shut down her computer, locked the house, and took the key with him.

He knew she was already in the air to Spokane, and wouldn't answer her phone regardless. On his way he took the risk of calling Cail, got his own voice mail. He didn't leave a message. It was nearly six-thirty.

The phone rang almost immediately and he glanced at it, decided to take a risk. "Yeah."

"It's Cail. I can't keep this up much longer. I think he's getting suspicious. What's going on?"

Brodey paused, carefully wording his answer. "I need to track her."

"Do you know where she's going?"

"I can't tell you that."

Cail hesitated. "You have an idea."

"I can't tell you that either. "

"Understood. What can you tell me?"

Brodey thought it out for a moment. Anything he told Cail, Ain would find out. And he couldn't lie to his brothers any more than they could lie to him. "I went to her house, she was gone. She left. I don't know exactly where she's going, although I think I can find her. It won't do Ain any good to go to her house because I took what I needed to track her. He's going to have to sit back and pray to the Goddess I can talk her into coming home if I find her."

It was Cail's turn to play it cautious. "Don't tell me any more than that."

"Right. I can't promise I'll call you or text you again."

"Try to do something when you find her, let me know she's okay."

"I'll do that. Text me immediately when he edicts you. That way I'll know not to play voicemails." Brodey hung up and turned the phone off. From this point on, he was incommunicado.

He stopped at a Wal-Mart in Sarasota and bought two disposable phones, along with plenty of minutes for them, and activated both. He didn't want to risk the number coming from Spokane and Ain tracking it. Three hours later he was in the air and ordering a scotch on the rocks from the flight attendant manning the drink cart.

He pulled Elain's ring from his pocket and looked at it, fighting his tears. He couldn't lose her. He also knew he would never agree to Ain forcing her to stay, either. He loved her too much, wanted her to be happy. Even if that happiness wasn't with them.

What she didn't understand is that now that they had mated and marked her, there was no breaking their bond with her.

Only death could do that.

They might not be with her, but now they couldn't be with anyone else, either.

He allowed himself a few minutes to mentally bitch and moan, then started flipping through her entire address book. Stupid, he didn't even know what her mother's name was or where she lived. Ain had been too worried about chaining Elain to them to even find that kind of shit out. No wonder she took off. Frankly, he couldn't blame her.

He found three names with Spokane addresses, all couples from the looks of the entries. None with Elain's last name. Then a fourth, and he knew he'd hit the jackpot.

(Mom) Carla Taylor, 859 E. Falls Hill Dr., Spokane.

And the phone number.

He closed his eyes and took a long, deep, relieved breath.

* * * *

Ain didn't know what was going on. Cail worked in his study with the door closed. Brodey had disappeared somewhere, and Elain wasn't around either.

By seven-thirty, when neither Elain nor Brodey had returned, Ain knocked on Cail's study door.

"Come in."

Ain opened the door. Cail was hunched over his computer, the accounting software up, the business checkbook open on the desk next to him, as well as stacks of receipts and invoices piled to the side.

"What's going on?" Ain asked him.

"Hmm? What?"

Cail's voice sounded too tight, too edgy. Both Brodey and Cail had given him the cold shoulder for most of the day.

Treading carefully, not wanting to piss him off again after the morning's exchange, Ain asked, "Are we fending for ourselves tonight for dinner? Or is Elain going to cook?"

Cail didn't turn to face him. He shrugged. "I guess we're fending for ourselves. I know there are leftovers in there to finish off."

Ain studied his brother's back. The tension rolled off him.

"What's going on?" Ain quietly asked.

Cail still didn't turn. "I want to get the accounts in order. I've been slacking the past few days. I'm behind in my bookkeeping."

"That's not what I mean." Looking at Cail's back was really starting to piss him off. "What's going on? Where are Brodey and Elain?"

"I don't know."

"*Tell* me where they are."

"I. Don't. Know."

* * * *

Fuck! Prime edict. Thank the Goddess he *didn't* know!

"Did they tell you where they went?" Ain growled.

Cail breathed another mental sigh of relief. "Nope, they didn't."

He felt Ain's presence directly behind him. "Did they tell you when they were coming back?"

"Nope." He tried to focus as he entered another receipt into the software.

"Did they go somewhere together?"

"Not that I'm aware of. Brodey left while you were in the shower."

"And you don't know where he is?"

"Nope."

He heard Ain turn and mutter under his breath. A moment later, Cail glanced down at his lap where Brodey's phone lay. It lit up, Ain's cell number on the screen.

Cail smiled. Sometimes Brodey could be smart when he tried.

He heard Ain in the living room. "Brodey, give me a call when you get this. I'd like to know where the hell you and Elain are."

Another silent sigh of relief from Cail. No edict.

Please find her, Brod, Cail thought. *Please find her and keep her safe and talk her into coming home.* If anyone could sweet talk her, it was Brodey.

Chapter Four

Elain thought the tightness in her chest would get better as they lifted off from TIA. It didn't get worse, but it settled deeper, right between her lungs. She'd managed to get a window seat and stared down at the Gulf of Mexico as they winged their way toward Washington State. Would Ain track her down? The station wouldn't give out her personal information, she knew that. They were the only ones Ain could pump for possible info about her. He could hire a private investigator but that would take time to find her.

Maybe Cail and Brodey would keep him off her ass for a while.

She didn't want to stay out there indefinitely. She also knew as soon as she returned home to Venice that Ain would be on her like white on rice, ordering her back to Arcadia. Not that she didn't want to be there.

She just didn't want to be there with *him*.

Poor Brodey and Cail. She closed her eyes and tried not to cry as she thought about their faces, how upset they'd be. Worse, she knew she loved Ain. For him to treat her like that when she trusted him, it felt like her insides had been ripped out.

She didn't call her mom, she'd surprise her.

It was after eight o'clock local time when the plane touched down in Spokane. Elain rented a car and thought about turning her phone on, then reconsidered it. She'd need to get another phone. She couldn't play her voicemails from the boys.

Her boys. She already thought of them as hers.

She had to let them go.

* * * *

Her mom was pleasantly shocked by her arrival. When Carla stepped back she looked Elain in the eye. "What's wrong?"

Elain tried to smile but broke down sobbing. Carla led her inside to the sofa and sat, holding Elain until she cried the story out.

Well, most of it. Leaving out the parts about getting it on with all three men, and the fact that they were shape-shifters, and she'd only known them approximately two weeks and was now mated to them.

And then the new, crazy mood swings that made her feel like an alien in her own skin. She'd never in her entire life been so emotionally volatile.

"So he asked you to marry him and wants you to quit your job?"

Elain sniffled. Close enough. "Yeah. I heard him talking to his brothers this morning. He told me one line and told them something else."

"Then don't quit."

I wish it was that easy! "I love th—him so much." *Whew, almost screwed up there.*

"Have you had anything to eat?"

Elain shook her head.

Carla nudged her into sitting up. "Let's get you some food, kiddo. I've got some leftover mac and ham in the fridge from last night. How long are you staying?"

Forever? A deep, sharp pang hit her when she thought that. *Damn edict.* She'd have to figure a loophole around that.

"I took a few days off. I wanted some time and distance to think."

"Does he know where you are?"

"No. I didn't tell him I was leaving."

Carla frowned. "Are you afraid of him? Is he abusive?"

"No!" She recognized her mother's skeptical frown. "No, Mom, seriously. He's just...very old fashioned." She took a deep breath. "He's not abusive, I swear. Do you honestly think I'd put up with that? He just doesn't like the idea of me driving two hours a day to work and back."

"What does he expect you to do? Stay home barefoot and pregnant?"

Elain shook her head again. "No. He said he would like to have kids one day, but when or if is up to me."

Carla set a heaping plate of macaroni and cheese with chopped ham in front of Elain. "Well, two hours a day in a car does seem like a lot. He's not willing to move into your place?"

"It's a working cattle ranch. He can't."

She nodded. "Oh. He expects you to stay there and keep house and work on the farm, so to speak?"

"No, that's not what he said."

"What did he say?"

She couldn't exactly tell her that. "He just said he didn't like the idea of me driving two hours a day."

"He didn't forbid you from working?"

Elain shoveled another forkful of pasta into her mouth and shook her head. Technically he hadn't.

"I'm guessing Arcadia doesn't have a TV station you could go to work for."

Elain snorted. "Not quite."

By the time Elain polished off her second plate of macaroni it was nearly ten o'clock local time, and she felt totally exhausted. It would be after midnight at home, and the boys would be...

Frantic.

She felt a guilty pang that she couldn't call them, at least Cail and Brodey, to tell them she was okay.

* * * *

Brodey's plane touched down after midnight local time. He rented a car and, with map in hand, drove immediately to the address.

Two cars parked in the driveway, no lights on in the house.

He drove around the block and parked on a side street, then walked back to the house. No one around, no street lights. The driveway was two cars wide but the second car had been parked directly behind the first. He walked over to the driver's side and smelled.

He wanted to weep with relief and fought the urge to bang on the front door and demand to see Elain. Definitely not how to handle this.

He touched the car, stroked the handle where she'd touched it. He brought his hand to his face and deeply inhaled.

Something that had tensed inside his gut relaxed.

Elain was with her mom, she wasn't in any danger. He had to let her be. For tonight, at least.

He closed his eyes and sent his mind out, wondered if she could sense him. He found her, thankfully asleep. Even asleep he felt her anguish, her pain.

Her agony.

Her broken heart.

Then he did cry. They'd hurt her. Yes, it was Ain's fault, not his, but he was as responsible as his brothers for her well-being. Code of the Ancients decreed that shifters kept their mates happy and protected.

He forced himself to walk back to his car and drive to a nearby hotel. He could talk to her in the morning and apologize.

Hopefully make amends.

* * * *

Ain paced, angrily muttering. At nine o'clock he stormed into the study.

"*Look* at me," he growled.

Cail turned. He'd already slipped the phone into his pocket. *Here we go, Prime edict time.*

"*Where* are they?"

"I told you, I don't know where they are."

"You know something. You're not telling me something. *What* are you not telling me? *Tell me!*"

Cail opened his email program and brought up the email, then stood so Ain could sit. "Congratulations, asshole, you managed to run her off. Brodey found her ring where she'd left it in the middle of the kitchen table."

Ain sat and read the note for several long minutes. Cail expected the yelling and screaming to start at any time.

He wasn't prepared for Ain's soft, sad whisper. "Oh, no."

Cail snorted, disgusted. "Oh, yes."

"Did Brodey…"

"Brodey went after her. He went to her house first, and no, he didn't tell me what he found or where he suspected she might go. He knew you would edict me. All he said was she wasn't there, she obviously wasn't going back there soon, and he'd taken what he needed to find her with him."

Ain didn't take his eyes off the screen. "She ran away?" he softly asked.

"Excellent. You get the slow on the uptake award." He punched him, hard, in the back of the shoulder. "Thanks a lot, Mr. Prime Asshole. This is all your fucking fault."

Cail stormed out of the study and left Ain sitting there. At least now he could take a fucking shower. He stripped and tossed his clothes on the floor and stood under water as hot as he could stand it.

When he finished twenty minutes later, Ain still sat in the study with the email up. Cail went over to give him another piece of his mind. When he spun the chair around the words died in his mouth.

Ain was crying.

"I don't deserve her," Ain softly said. "I don't deserve her at all."

Even as pissed as Cail felt, he was hard pressed to kick his brother when he looked that far down.

"You have got to give in some. You need to apologize to her, if Brodey can find her and make her listen to him, and tell her she can keep working if that's what she wants. This punitive edict shit has got to stop. I can understand and agree with protocol shit around shifters, sure, but not for stuff like this when she's still trying to wrap her head around everything. I mean, this is a fairly trippy mind fuck for her to begin with. Then you go all Neanderthal on her and mess with her. She barely knows us!"

Ain sadly nodded. "Yeah."

"I would suggest you also lift the edict about her living here."

Ain looked horrified. Cail cut off his protests. "You read her note. She doesn't trust you. I'm not saying it won't fucking be misery on all of us. You have got to prove to her you're serious. You have to reearn her trust. Let her come back to us when she's ready. You said yourself you didn't want to force her, and that's basically what you're doing. You know as well as I do it won't take long for her to come back if you just leave her the hell alone."

After a long moment, Ain's shoulders slumped. "You're right."

"Please don't edict me into giving you updates. Because I'm not going to ask Brod where he is if he finds her."

Ain stood and shook his head. "No." The forlorn, sad tone of Ain's voice softened Cail's anger. "No more edicts. I'm done. I don't deserve her. I made her miserable. I violated the Code." He choked up. "Please tell her I lift all the edicts and I'm sorry I hurt her. Tell her I love her, that I'll always love her. And tell Brodey good-bye for me." He walked out the back door.

When Cail fully processed what Ain had said, he hurried after his brother. Ain had already shifted, left his clothes on the porch, and disappeared into the night.

"Fuck!" Cail screamed.

Chapter Five

Ain ran. He cleared his mind and tried to focus only on the scents and sounds of the night around him and not the deep burning ache in his heart.

His One. And he'd acted like an asshole and hurt her. After centuries alone, centuries of searching, he'd found her, and in less than two weeks managed to hurt her. The person he was supposed to take care of and devote his life to making happy, and he'd managed to screw everything up.

Brodey and Cailean warned him. They tried, Goddess bless 'em, to make him see sense. He'd been too stupid and stubborn to listen. He wanted to do the right thing and keep her there with them, safe, so they could make her happy. He thought she'd want that, would feel the pull the way they did, would want to be with them.

From the start he'd made a mess of the whole situation. He didn't want to force her to be with them, he'd promised that from the beginning, but wasn't that exactly what he'd done?

They'd be better off without him. *She* would be better off without him.

She would be *happy* without him. Brodey and Cail could take care of her far better than he ever could. They understood her more than he did, obviously.

Problem was, there was only one way to break the bond.

He choked back a sob that, had anyone else heard, would have sounded like a howl.

He ran.

* * * *

Cail paced. By midnight, Ain still hadn't returned. Deep in Cail's gut he suspected Ain wouldn't. Cail shifted and tried to track him, but with all the fairly fresh scents he lost him and had to turn back to the house.

"FUCK!" He brought Ain's clothes inside and dumped them on the coffee table. He pulled on shorts and went to go get Brodey's phone when Ain's pants rang.

Goddess, could this night get any more fucked up? He fished Ain's phone out of the pocket and looked at the screen. It was Xavier, their barn manager.

"What?"

"Aindreas? I've been trying to call you."

"This is Cail. What's wrong?"

"You see the weather report tonight on the news?"

"No, what?"

"They upgraded that tropical storm late this evening, the one out in the Gulf, Natalia. The National Hurricane Center, it's projecting landfall around Venice and then coming straight across Arcadia."

"Aw FUCK!" He sooo did not need this. Hurricane Charley had really screwed things up for a long time. They'd only just gotten the last barn rebuilt two years before.

"Sorry. I need to know what you want me to do. We've got three days until landfall, and they're predicting a Cat 3 storm."

Cail groaned. The good news just kept dumping on top of him. "Okay, call all the guys, I'll be over there in a few minutes, let me get some coffee. We need to bring them all in to pasture two, and we need to get the calves and any pregnant cows into the reinforced barn."

"I figured, but I wanted to call and find out for sure."

"Thanks." Cail hung up and took a deep breath as he walked into the kitchen and started a pot of coffee. No sleep for him tonight. At least he could get Brodey to come back, hopefully with Elain.

Then again, with a storm on the way, maybe she should stay wherever she was, hopefully safe and sound and one less worry on his plate. He started the coffee, tried calling his cell phone.

Voicemail. "Hey, dude, call me immediately. Major shitstorm here and I don't mean Ain. He's lifted the edicts, but he's shifted and disappeared and we've got a Cat 3 hurricane on the way. I need you home, right the fuck now." He hung up and sent a text message.

SAFE TO CALL, NO EDICTS, CALL ME NOW EMERGENCY!
Send.

He switched Brodey's phone to normal mode so he could hear it, then pocketed both it and Ain's phones. After he filled a large Thermos with coffee, Cail grabbed his keys and headed out the back door to get a work truck.

* * * *

Elain spent a restless night in her mom's guest room. At one point she dreamed of Brodey standing in the yard below and calling to her. A dream so realistic it woke her up. She even got out of bed and walked over to the window. Of course she saw nothing.

She tried and failed to go back to sleep. How could it feel so damn right after just a few days, sleeping cuddled with all of them, and then so wrong to sleep alone? Like part of her soul had been ripped out of her.

The next morning, Carla made her scrambled eggs and bacon and toast. She didn't push Elain to speak, and let the Today Show fill in with background noise.

Elain eventually broke her silence. "What do I do?"

"I can't tell you that, honey."

"I don't want to lose him. He's a good man." That was the truth. Despite her anger, she knew Ain's heart, had felt his love for her. He wasn't trying to be malicious, just trying to be a good Prime. With a little distance between them and time for her anger to cool just a smidge, she could see that.

"Maybe you two can work it out. You could try to call him. He's probably worried about you."

Going fucking batshit was probably closer to the truth. "Maybe later." She still hadn't turned on her phone, worried what she might see.

Worried about calls she might not see. What if the boys let her go without trying to talk her into coming home?

What if they didn't really give a shit, and this had all been one big mind fuck?

It was close to eight o'clock after she helped her mom do the dishes. She started for the stairs so she could take her shower when the doorbell rang.

"Who the hell is that?" her mom asked.

But Elain knew. She felt it in her gut. *Brodey.*

She raced across the living room and beat her mom to the front door, threw it open.

There he stood, his green eyes sad and mournful.

Before he could say anything she launched herself at him, sobbing.

He wrapped his arms around her and whispered to her, trying to soothe her, apologizing.

"Remember to call me Ain, babe," he mentally reminded her.

She nearly asked out loud. *"Why?"*

"Because it'll be hard to explain why you go upstairs and bop your fiancé's brother."

"Good thinking." She stepped back and looked at him. "How did you find me?"

"Long story. Please let me apologize and beg and grovel and give you whatever you want to get you to come back?"

"Get extra heapings of begging and groveling out of him," Carol snarked from behind her.

Elain laughed and sniffled, then stepped back and grabbed Brodey's hand. "Mom, this is…Aindreas. Aindreas Lyall." Damn, it felt weird calling him that.

Brodey nodded and stuck out his right hand. "I'm sorry this meeting is under such bad circumstances, ma'am."

"My daughter shows up at my house after flying across the country, sobbing her eyes out over a man. Don't expect me to think too highly of you right now, son."

He nodded. "Agreed. I acted like a jerk. I swear I won't ever be like that again. I love her. I'll do whatever I have to do to win her back."

Carla sighed. "I suppose you two should go upstairs to talk or kiss and make up or make out or whatever you're going to do. I have about an hour's worth of gardening to do outside. Good luck." She turned and headed for the backyard.

Elain wanted to drag Brodey upstairs right then, but he held back. "No, babe, please. Let's talk." He led her to the couch and wrapped his arms around her. "I'm so sorry. I can't say it enough."

She cried again. "You didn't do anything wrong, Brodey. It's all *his* fault." With Brodey in her arms the ache had returned with a vengeance for the two missing men. And what little equanimity she'd regained with her emotions vaporized.

"I'm just as responsible for your happiness as he is. I should have fought more. Cail and I both should have. It's in the Code."

"So how long before he shows up? Or," she bitterly added, "are you supposed to drag me home by my hair?"

He kissed her, long and deep and sweet. She knew she'd let him drag her home by her hair without a fight if he wanted to. Then he told her the story and she smiled.

"I guess that makes us exiles, huh?"

He laughed. "Babe, I don't give a shit what it makes us as long as I've got you in my arms again."

* * * *

Brodey went upstairs with Elain to take a shower. She eagerly pulled him into the bathroom. He quickly stripped and stepped inside the shower with her, kissed her.

"I love you, babe. Goddess, I'm so glad I found you!"

Elain had to admit she was pretty glad he'd found her, too. He slid his hands down her body as they stood under the water, his cock quickly inflating. His fingers slipped between her legs and she moaned into his mouth as he kissed her.

She also knew, regardless of how pissed she was at Aindreas, she would most likely end up back on the cattle ranch in Arcadia with her three men. She might be giving his royal Primeness the cold shoulder for a while—a long while—but it hurt too much not to be with them.

All of them.

Even Ain.

Brodey pushed a thick finger inside her and she moaned louder, rocking her hips against his hand, trying to get traction against her clit. She wouldn't deny the sex was amazing.

He cradled her with his other arm, and pressed his lips to the top of her head. "Come for me, baby. Give it to me."

She held onto his shoulders and closed her eyes as he stroked her closer to release. When she came, she bit down on his shoulder to muffle her cries, drawing a low, needy hiss from him. Then he pinned her against the wall and slid inside her ready entrance, locking his lips onto hers as he buried himself balls-deep inside her.

"Oh, baby!" he mentally sighed.

She had to admit the psychic connection shit was pretty cool, too.

He closed his eyes and slowly thrust, savoring it. *"I missed you so much, baby. I was so worried."*

She hooked her legs around him and he cupped his hands under her ass, lifting her, fully impaling her on his stiff shaft.

"I'm sorry I scared you."

He broke their kiss to nuzzle her neck. "I love you, sweetheart," he whispered against her flesh. "Please come home with me. I won't force you. I won't make you. But please, think about it?"

She nodded. "Yes."

He kissed her again and thrust home, hard, exploding inside her with a low growl.

When they recovered he held her under the water, caressing her, reluctant to let her go. After they finished he toweled her off, kissing her flesh.

"No matter what I have to do, babe," he softly promised, "I'll stand up to him. He loves you. He just...he doesn't understand. He's letting what he thinks he has to do get in the way of common fricking sense."

"I know."

He kissed her again and they got dressed. "Oh, can I please put this back where it belongs?" He held up the ring.

She nodded. He took her hand, slid the ring onto her finger.

"I love you," he said. "I'll do anything I can to make you happy."

She handed him her BlackBerry. "Will you please check my phone for me?"

He smiled and took it. When he turned it on, a flurry of text messages and voicemails came through. He looked at the call log and frowned.

"What? Is he that mad?"

He shook his head. "They're from the station. Your boss."

She frowned and took the phone. She groaned when she listened to the messages, four of them, from Danny.

"What?"

She hit replay and handed him the phone.

"Hey, Elain, this is Danny. I hate to do this to you, but all vacations and days off are canceled, you can make it up next week. NHC just upped Natalia. It's show time. Call me."

Brodey grabbed Cail's phone and turned it on. The text message showed up immediately.

Brodey called his phone and anxiously waited for Cail to answer. He finally did. "Hey, I'm with her—"

"Fine, now shut up. Dude, I need you home. Now."

"Yeah, I heard about the storm."

"No, dude, not just the storm." Cail hesitated. "He's gone."

* * * *

Cail stared at Ain's pile of clothes still laying on the coffee table. He hadn't had time to pick things up.

"Gone?" Brodey asked. "What do you mean he's gone? Ain's gone?"

"He left last night. He edicted me into admitting she'd left. I showed him the email. He..." Cail blew out a deep breath. "I don't think he's planning on coming back. He told me to tell her he loves her, that he's lifted all the edicts. He shifted, Brod. He left, and I can't find him."

"Fuck."

"And with this storm, I need you home. As in the next flight home. We've got two thousand cows about to fly over the fucking moon unless I can get them rounded up. I need you here. I can't cut them by myself, and I can't shift to work them without you here."

"All right. We'll go to the airport now."

"Can I speak to her?"

"Hold on."

It sounded like he handed the phone over. Then Elain's tentative voice. "Cail?"

He closed his eyes, relieved. "Babe. It's good to hear your voice."

"What's going on? Where's Ain?"

"I don't know sweetheart. Let's get you guys back here and we can talk about that later."

"No, we'll talk about it now!"

Cail knew he had to be firm with her. "Honey, I don't *know* where he is. He dropped the edicts, we can sort out the rest later. Right now, I've got two thousand head of cattle I need to move and I need Brodey's help. I've got to get back out there. Please be careful coming home. Okay? I love you." As much as he wanted her safe and out of the storm's path, he wanted her home even more.

"I love you too, Cail."

He hung up. Of all the fucking times for Ain to decide *not* to be a prick Prime, this was not the best one.

It was going to be a long fucking day.

Cail tried not to focus on Ain. Not with all the preparations ahead of him. Not just the livestock, but the house had to be boarded up, equipment had to be moved into the barns…

If he tried to think about it all, he'd lose his mind.

Priority—cattle.

He refilled his Thermos with coffee and headed outside.

* * * *

Brodey held her while she cried. "It's okay, babe."

"No, it's not okay. I didn't want him to leave! I just wanted him to not be an asshole." She'd managed to regain a little mental stability, but the news that Ain was missing had sent her on another crying jag. *What the hell is wrong with me?*

"I know." He patted her on the back and got her to sit up. "We need to go."

She quickly packed her things and led him downstairs, left him in the living room while she walked out back to find her mom. He studied pictures on the bookshelf, of a younger Elain with Carla. From college graduation to Elain earning a black belt in karate as a teenager, winning ribbons in track meets, down to adorable toddler, but no pictures of her as an actual baby.

No pictures of a man, either. Just Elain and her mom.

Odd. He didn't have time to think about it right then.

The women returned a moment later. Carla still looked standoffish and he felt a decidedly chilly wall around her.

"You're sure you want to go back to Florida with him?" Carla asked.

"I'm sorry, Mom. I hate popping in and out like this, but it's my job. It's a big story."

Carla shook her finger at Brodey and glared. "When I get down there, you'd better be taking good care of my little girl!"

He smiled. "Yes, ma'am. I sure will, I promise. I'm sorry I acted like a jerk."

He loaded Elain's things into her car for her. "I'll follow you to the airport."

Two hours later, they caught a flight back to Tampa. On the plane he laced his fingers through hers, relieved for the moment, trying not to worry about Ain. This was Ain's fault. If he wanted to be an asshole and play Houdini, that was his problem, not theirs.

He feathered his lips across her knuckles. "Are you okay, babe?"

"Yeah. I can't quit thinking about Ain."

"He's a big boy. He'll come back after he blows off some steam."

"He lied to me. I can't believe he lied to me."

"He didn't lie to you. He can't lie to you."

She glared at him.

"Seriously. Yeah, I know, he acted like an asshole and played a mind game, yes. But we can't lie to you."

"What do you mean?"

He shrugged. "We can't lie to each other, and now that you're our mate, we can't lie to you, either. It's part of the Code. We're bound."

"When do I get to learn more about this stupid Code?"

"Once you settle down long enough we can start teaching you, sweetie. And you can't lie to us, either. It's just one of those things."

"I wouldn't lie to you guys. I'm not into mind fucks like Mr. Prime."

He needed to distract her, she was getting pissed off again. "Tell me about your mom and dad."

"Mom." He looked at her questioningly and she continued. "I'm adopted. My birth mother died when I was about a year old. My mom and her were best friends. When she found out she was dying, she gave my mom—Carla—custody of me."

"No grandparents?"

Elain shook her head. "Only Mom's. My birth mother's parents were killed when she was sixteen or something. I don't know anything about them. She didn't talk to my mom much about her family."

"What about your father?"

Elain shrugged. "I don't know him. Apparently my mom only knew his name, didn't know how to find him. He knew my birth mother was pregnant. He disappeared about a month after she found out I would be a girl."

"Carla didn't change your last name when she adopted you?"

"My birth mom gave me my father's last name in case he ever came around looking for me." She bitterly laughed. "Not much chance of that. My mom told me she only met the guy once and he was a real charmer. Some Irish guy named Liam." She smiled at Brodey. "Maybe that's why I've got a thing for guys with accents."

He waggled his eyebrows at her and softly said, "Frrrreeddoom!" making sure to roll the Rs.

It had the desired effect. She laughed.

"You grew up in Spokane?" he asked.

"No. Born and raised in Tampa. Mom moved out to Spokane a few years ago, after she retired, because her family's from there. I was already working and didn't want to move." She looked sad. "I miss her not being closer."

He kissed her temple. "We could always move out there."

"What are you talking about?"

Brodey shrugged. "Sell out, move. We can do something

somewhere else. Trust me, babe, there's more than enough money stored up for that to easily happen."

"What haven't you guys told me yet?"

"We told you we have money. You don't live as long as we do without amassing some major moolah unless you're a total dumbass."

"And you guys aren't dumbasses."

He shrugged, then grinned. "Not about that, at least."

She rested her head against his shoulder for most of the flight. "You know what's really stupid?" she asked after an hour of silence.

He kissed the top of her head. He could sit there like that with her forever. "What, babe?"

"I reeeeaaallly don't want to go to work. A huge story, the kind I live for, and all I want to do is go home with you."

He kissed her again. "They need you. We'll still be there when the storm's over."

"You don't mind?"

"It's not my call. I'm not willing to make you unhappy. My preference is to have you safe with us, not trotting around in a storm. I'm going to worry my ass off about you every second you're out of my sight, so will Cail. I also know if it's what you need to be happy, I can't deny you."

She met his eyes. "I love you. But I love my job and what I do. I worked really hard to get where I am."

"I know. If you stay at the station, though, then we have to keep our relationship on the back burner."

"What do you mean?"

"We can't be seen with you in public, can't make it known."

"Even if I'm not on air?"

He sadly shook his head.

"Why not?"

He arched his eyebrows and dropped his voice. "Honey, triplet shape-shifters who don't age? *You* won't age. We can't be seen together while you're working for the station. Too much risk, people would ask questions. We'll have to postpone the wedding—"

"No!"

He nodded. "Yes," he sadly whispered. "You know I'm right. It doesn't mean we can't be together sometimes in private. Let's face it, that's a long fucking drive for you every day. I don't want you on the road that much. It doesn't make sense to make you live in Arcadia, and he's dropped the edict about you living at the ranch."

"Can't...can't you guys stay with me?"

He shrugged. "Sure, sometimes. Not all of us, because usually one of us needs to be back home to oversee things. It's rare that all three of us leave at the same time for more than a day or so. We can swap out on the weekends or something."

He knew it was mean to be so blunt, but better to be honest like this than the mind games Ain tried to play with her.

She looked stunned. He kissed her hand again. "Babe, Cail and I will never force you to choose between your job and us. We *will* be waiting for you when you're ready to take the next step. I know Cail will back me up on this."

"What about Ain?"

He shrugged, not wanting to give voice to his thoughts. "I doubt he'll overrule us this time."

Chapter Six

When they arrived back in Tampa, Brodey refused to let Elain carry her own bag. He helped her out to her car and she drove him to his truck. Before they split up, he tightly hugged her and kissed her again.

"Be safe, babe," he said. "Call us, keep us updated on how you are during the storm. Focus on your job so you don't get hurt, okay?"

"I will."

He buried his face in her hair and inhaled. "I'll spank your ass myself if I see video of you standing out in the middle of the wind and rain, got it?" he growled.

She laughed. "I won't do that. I promise. You be safe, too."

"Yeah. Don't panic if we don't answer, just leave us voicemails. Sometimes it's fastest to move cattle shifted, so we might not have pants."

"I must really be in love if I can accept all this crazy mess."

* * * *

Ain ran all day. He didn't pay attention to where he was, vaguely recognized he'd headed south. He didn't want to know, didn't want to think or feel.

Didn't want to hurt.

He curled up under a vacant mobile home and slept at some point in the afternoon and dreamed of Elain. When he awoke near dark, he was hungry and thirsty and sore all over from his journey.

He waited to crawl from his hiding spot until dark. The nearby road looked like a good option. No lights, no stop signs or signals, the kind of road rated for fifty-five that people usually blew down a lot faster.

It would be quick.

He sat in the ditch, his black coat hidden in the shadowy gloom, and waited.

* * * *

They drove south on I-75, Brodey following her. When they passed the exit for Arcadia, Elain felt a pang when she looked in her rear view mirror and watched Brodey's truck swing off toward the ramp.

She gripped her steering wheel and fought the urge to slam on the brakes and drive off the road to follow him. She'd already called her boss and told him she was on the way. It would be a busy couple of days. The NHC seemed fairly certain about their projected track, landfall somewhere between Punta Gorda and Sarasota. With no weather fronts to steer Hurricane Natalia elsewhere, they were down to a waiting game. County officials from Lee to Manatee County scrambled to finalize their mandatory evacuation orders.

Elain stopped by her house and rolled down the shutters. Thank God she had them, it made the job super-fast and easy. Then she repacked her overnight bag, grabbed a few things for her comfort. It would be days before she made it home. She might have to shower at the station, depending on how the storm moved.

Her boss, Danny, pounced almost the minute she walked in the door. "There you are! Great. Conference room, right now."

She tried to keep her mind on the meeting. Danny handed out rain gear and other supplies to the crews. Bill, the photojournalist she usually worked with, plopped into the chair next to her.

"Glad to see you back. Where you been?"

"Needed some time off."

She felt his eyes on her. He'd been with her that day at the Arcadia Highland Games when Brodey jumped into their news van. *Jesus, barely two weeks ago!* she was startled to realize.

His eyes nearly burned a hole in her back. She finally turned to look at him. "What, Bill?" They'd worked together for four years, first running cameras, and now with him filming her. They'd gone to college together before that.

"You look different."

"Different how?"

He shook his head. "I don't know. Like you've changed."

Buddy, you have no fucking clue. "I'm fine. I'm very tired. I just flew in from Spokane."

"No, it's not that. It's...I don't know how to explain it." He grinned. "Did you meet a guy?"

She hoped she didn't blush. "My personal life is none of your fucking business."

"Ah ha! I knew it! You got laid." He was the only one she'd ever let talk to her like that, the banter no different than what they'd had between them for years.

And yet now it felt totally wrong. *Like I should ask the boys to beat the crap out of him for me.*

She mentally gasped. This was her friend!

"Drop it, Bill," she growled.

Danny started the meeting, handed out assignments. Elain didn't protest when she found out she'd be covering DeSoto county.

Arcadia.

Home.

"See if you can find a local rancher," Danny said. "Do a story about their livestock preparations, maybe tie it in to what happened during Hurricane Charley or something."

She reddened, her heart racing with excitement. "Okay. I'll call the Lyall brothers." Her heart pounded. She could be with her boys!

Bill snickered. "Isn't that the guy who owned the dog?"

She hoped she didn't blush too badly. "Yeah."

"I'll send you two out with a big truck and Carl, the engineer," Danny said. "It shouldn't be as bad inland as it will be here. I want one of the big trucks away from the coast, try to protect it."

She nodded. "Okay."

"Cool! I get to play with the big toys!" Bill said with a grin.

It was dark when Bill, Carl and Elain finished loading their stuff in the microwave truck and stopped at Wal-Mart for some non-perishable supplies. Elain was on her last nerve. They'd already arranged for hotel rooms in Arcadia for the night even though she suspected she might end up with her boys.

She hoped Ain had returned, but with Carl and Bill there, she couldn't call to check.

* * * *

Ain saw the approaching headlights and took a deep breath. They wouldn't see him, and they were moving too fast to stop in time.

For her, he thought. For her happiness. If Elain wasn't bound to him, she could be happy.

He stepped into the middle of the lane and sat, closed his eyes, and waited.

Hopefully it wouldn't hurt too much.

* * * *

"Lester, slow down!" Mabel couldn't drive at night anymore, hadn't been able to for years. She didn't think Lester should be driving at night either, but they'd stayed at bingo longer than usual, listening to Lora Jean's story about her daughter's appendectomy.

"Speed limit's fifty-five. I'm doing thirty. How much slower you want me to go?"

She hated the tiny car, their son's idea. The smart fortwo, a car that made a Ford Escort look like a Hummer by comparison. How could you take a car seriously that was not only tinier than a VW Bug, but spelled without capital letters? When gas prices had shot through the roof, their son had made them trade in their Cadillac for the tiny thing. Yes, it was a lot cheaper to run, and no, they didn't drive more than five miles from home, but she felt like she sat in a little tiny bubble.

Lester suddenly swore and hit the brakes. She looked up just as they heard the thump and a dark, furry shape went flying.

"Oh my God! What was that?" she screamed.

He pulled to the side. "A huge dog, just sitting in the middle of the road. Black. Didn't see the dang thing."

"Did you kill it?"

"I don't know, Mabel," he irately groused. "That's why I'm getting out." He put the emergency blinkers on and dragged himself out of the tiny car. He walked back a few yards and found it, a huge dog lying on the side of the road, still breathing.

"Be careful, Lester!" Mabel called from the car.

In a nearby house, a light went on outside and a man walked out. "What happened?"

Lester shook his head. "Is this your dog?"

The guy walked up. "No, never seen it before." He leaned over. "He's still alive." The man's wife had followed him outside. He called to her. "Honey, get me that old blanket from the garage."

Mabel walked up. "Oh, the poor thing!"

The dog lifted his head and looked at them before dropping it to the ground again.

The other man's wife brought the blanket. "My brother works for Animal Control. I'll call him and find out what to do with him. Maybe he's just stunned. I don't see any blood." He carefully wrapped the dog in the blanket. "Jeez, he's huge." He lifted him. "Unless you want to take him?"

Lester shook his head. "Our cat hates dogs. I hope he'll be okay."

* * * *

An hour before dark, Brodey arrived at the ranch. He found Cail in the southwestern pasture with Xavier, trying to round up cattle. Xavier was out on an ATV, its headlight cutting through the increasing gloom.

"Man, I am so fucking glad to see you," Cail said to him.

Brodey had shifted at the house and ran to join Cail. *"Any sign of Ain?"*

"No. I'm fucking worried too, but we've got too much to do to go looking for him."

"How do you want to handle this?"

"Run out and drive those heifers this way, towards Xavier. I've got the other crews working the east pasture. Make sure we didn't miss any strays, that's been the hardest part. I couldn't shift to see if we'd missed any."

"Gotcha." Brodey took off for the herd and started moving the cattle toward the gate. He loved running cattle. Any other day, or night, he'd be in heaven.

* * * *

As soon as Elain was alone in her room, she called Cail's cell and got voicemail. Then she tried Brodey. Cail answered.

"Babe, it's good to hear your voice. You okay?"

"Yeah. Is Ain back yet?"

"No, hon. Brodey's out in the pasture. I can't get him for you right now, he's shifted. Where are you?"

"You won't believe this." She told him.

His laugh warmed her heart. "You're right, I don't believe it, but I'm so fucking glad you have no idea. You guys can stay here tomorrow night and the day after. We've got room in the equipment barn by the house for the station's truck."

She recalled Brodey's admonishment. "Isn't that risky?"

"We won't be shifting in front of strangers, if that's what you mean. I'll feel a hell of a lot better having you here where I can be with you."

"We have to pretend you don't know me like that."

He laughed. "Funny, our dogs will love sleeping in your room with you."

She grinned. Cail and his loopholes. "Can you come by tonight?"

"I wish we could. We'll be busy until late tomorrow. I'm about to drop as it is, I've been up two days now. I need a nap at some point. Brodey will take over for me. Just come over tomorrow, any time. Okay?"

"Okay. Love you."

"Love you too, babe. Sleep tight."

Elain hung up and stared at her phone while fighting the urge to cry. She wanted to pound on the men's room door and demand the truck keys so she could drive out to the ranch right then.

She wanted to be with her men.

Well, two of them at least.

As she settled in to sleep, she couldn't help but worry about Ain.

* * * *

Bright light hurt Ain's eyes.

Gee, the bullshit was right about going to the light.

Ain forced an eye open and stared. He hurt all over and realized he was lying on some sort of exam table.

Well, obviously that *plan could have gone a little better.*

He felt hands on him, then heard a strange woman's voice. "You have it ready? I think he's coming to."

Another woman. "Yeah, hold on."

He felt something cold and wet on his front leg, wrinkled his nose at the sharp smell of alcohol.

He saw the hypo in her hand.

Oh, good. They're putting me to sleep. He breathed a sigh of relief. Maybe this wouldn't be so bad after all. They always said it didn't hurt when they euthanized animals.

He closed his eyes and relaxed as the drugs hit his system. He thought about Elain, her smile, her scent.

Her.

He loved her. He hoped wherever the Goddess deemed fit to send him in his next life that he could find happiness there, not fuck it up this time.

Everything faded to black.

The technician looked at the vet. "Okay. I've got the machine warmed up."

Working together, they carefully carried the large dog into the radiology room for X-rays.

A half-hour later, the vet studied the films. "He's got a couple of cracked ribs, probably a concussion. Other than that he looks like he's in good shape. No blood in his urine from the sample we drew."

She turned to the Animal Control officer. "He'll be okay when the sedative wears off. I'll give you some pain pills for him, it'll keep him calm and comfortable. What'll happen to him?"

"We're evaccing tomorrow morning. All animals go, even the mandatory holds. The only ones staying are two in quarantine for dog bite cases. Adoptables are being sent to Atlanta, the mandatory holds up to a shelter in Roanoke. Once it's safe we'll bring back the mandatories. If we have a shelter left standing."

The vet nodded and made a note in the chart. "We printed some extra pictures for you in case his owner comes looking for him. He's obviously well-loved. He's in great shape, well-fed. Definitely not a stray. I'd be willing to bet someone's looking for him. I'd keep him here but I'm already full from evacuation borders."

"No problem, doc. Thanks for coming in to look at him."

* * * *

Ain felt the pain first, deep and throbbing. It hurt to breathe, his head hurt.

Fuck. He wasn't dead yet.

He tried to lift his head and whined at the pain. Then two hands grabbed his muzzle. Before he could react, they shoved something in his mouth. The hands clamped down and stroked his chin.

A man's voice. "Swallow, boy."

He had to, or choke on the damn thing.

"That'll make you feel better while we transport you."

He started drifting again, happy to let whatever they'd given him take him away.

* * * *

The next morning at breakfast, Elain tried to curb her enthusiasm. "I talked to the Lyall brothers. Not only will they be happy to let us do a story on them and their storm prep, but they said we can ride the storm out at their place. And we can stash the truck in their barn."

Carl nodded. "That's cool. I'd hate to see the truck get beat up."

The storm still bore down, with Venice as the bull's-eye. Elain wanted to immediately set out for the Lyall ranch and knew she couldn't, she had to get her work done first.

They took several shots around Arcadia of plywood going up, some still painted with messages like "Go Away Charley" from several years earlier. They interviewed the DeSoto county administrator and emergency operations manager, filed those stories in time for the noon news. She tried not to think about Ain still missing. When she'd called and talked to Brodey that morning, they still hadn't heard anything from Ain.

She also fought to clamp down on her strange mood swings. From eagerness to get back to the ranch to irritation that their filming took so long, to anger and then sadness that Ain was missing.

Maybe I should cut down on the coffee.

Danny called. "Get a comment from Animal Control. I think they're clearing out the shelter."

Elain groaned. That would delay her getting to the ranch.

Getting home.

"Okay."

They pulled in a few minutes after eleven. One large truck towing a stock trailer pulled out as they pulled in. Another sat in the yard, being loaded with crates of dogs. She quickly located the shelter manager and they got some shots of animals being loaded for the trip.

"So what if someone's lost a pet? How would they go about claiming it?"

"Well, we've got pictures of all the animals being sent out, and we have tracking numbers for them all, so we can locate them. We'll have that information available after the storm. But we need the cage space for any animals displaced by the storm. Once everything's over, depending on whether or not the shelter's usable, we'll bring back as many as we can."

Elain filmed the story and they sent it to the station. She had to admit it was nice having the microwave truck for that.

They stopped for lunch, filmed some man on the street interviews, hit the local Wal-Mart and Publix to get shots of the lines of people buying supplies, then worked their way to the ranch. Carl drove and she fought the urge to demand he drive faster. The closer she got the more she felt the pull.

Her men.

Hers.

They pulled up in the yard at the house and her heart thumped at the sight of Brodey's truck. She wanted to jump out, run inside, and tackle them.

Her hands trembled from the exertion of not doing just that.

She led the way to the porch and the front door opened.

Cail.

He winked. *"Welcome home, babe."* "Nice to see you again, Ms. Pardie."

"Elain, please." *"You're a smartass."* "This is Bill and Carl."

The men shook hands. "Nice to meet you. Cailean Lyall." *"They aren't hitting on you, are they?"*

"Oh, please. Don't you start with me." "Thank you for allowing us to film your operations and for the generous offer of allowing us stay here." *"Behave yourself."*

"I'll behave. Brodey might pee on their bags, though." "Come on inside for a few minutes, bring your stuff, I'll show you to your rooms."

An hour later, Elain rode in the work truck with Cail while Carl and Bill followed them in the news truck.

Cail looked at her and grinned. "You don't know how badly I want to lean over and kiss you."

Her heart thumped in a pleasant way. "Kiss?"

He laughed. "Yeah, for starters. I'm so sorry, Elain. I'm with Brodey on this. We'll stand up to Ain, whatever we've got to do to make you happy, we'll do it."

"What happens when he edicts us again?"

Cail frowned. "I don't think he's going to do that again. Not for stuff like this."

"Is he okay?"

"I don't know." He reached across the seat and held her hand. At least that was safe enough to do with the other vehicle following. "I hope so."

They spent the afternoon filming. Brodey raced across the pasture from where he was helping Xavier and some of the men with the last of the cattle. He jumped up on her and licked her cheek.

"Oh, Goddess, you're a sweet sight!"

"Hi...Beta. Good boy." *"You too, honey."*

Bill laughed. "He still likes you."

She rubbed Brodey's head and stared into his eyes. "He's a good boy."

Brodey's tongue happily lolled.

"Go back to work before you get in trouble," Elain told him.

He licked her face one more time and ran back to the pasture.

They spent a few hours filming, cut a couple of stories, made a live shot, and she interviewed Xavier instead of Cail at Cail's insistence. Brodey shifted back at some point and drove up in another truck.

She had a hard time keeping her mind on Ain with all the other stuff to do.

Now they were down to last-minute prep. They had to drive back into Arcadia for another interview with the emergency operations manager and sheriff, then back to the ranch after stopping at an open store. Most of the traditional storm supplies had been picked clean, but Elain bought some fresh items to cook them all a good dinner.

Bill and Carl helped Brodey and Cail finish boarding up the house while Elain made dinner. Thank goodness, because she wouldn't have to explain her familiarity with the kitchen.

While dinner cooked, she spotted Ain's clothes on the coffee table. She walked over and picked them up with every intention of taking them into the bedroom, but put them to her face and deeply inhaled.

Clear as day, his image appeared in her mind.

She fought the urge to cry.

Yes, she was pissed at him. But after Cail told her what happened when she left, now she worried about Ain, prayed they could find him, kiss and make up.

Chapter Seven

Ain lost track of time. Vaguely aware of voices, being moved, the sound and smell of other animals around him, and pain.

If this is the afterlife, I'm soooo fucking screwed.

At one point he felt the world shift and tip and he whined in pain.

"Hold on." A woman's voice.

He heard something, opened his eyes in time to have his mouth pried open again, a pill shoved down his throat.

He swallowed.

"Good boy," she cooed.

He gave up. It didn't matter anymore. Without Elain, his life was worthless.

He drifted back to sleep.

* * * *

Ain didn't know how long he'd been asleep. He was aware of movement, being in a crate. At some point someone removed him from the crate and held a bowl of water in front of him. He drank but everything hurt. Where the fuck was he?

"Go potty, boy."

Screw it, his dignity was shot anyway. He relieved himself and whined as someone picked him up and put him back in the crate.

He escaped to sleep.

He awoke to darkness.

That's more like it.

He took a deep breath, felt the pain in his ribs, although the pain in his head seemed a little better.

He smelled animals, dogs and cats, but he wasn't moving anymore. They'd apparently reached their destination and he was in a building somewhere. Air conditioned.

He lifted his head and looked around. A shelter.

Fuck.

Where? That was the question.

He tried to stand and whined. Goddess, it fucking hurt! Leave it to him to fuck up his own suicide.

He wasn't in a crate anymore, but in a kennel run. Night time, wherever they were. The high windows in the wall revealed a starry sky.

He looked around and spotted the red light. *Fuck, video camera.*

That meant he couldn't shift.

He looked at the latch on the gate, hooked with a leash snap. Couldn't nose it open to escape.

He sighed. *Great.*

He slowly hauled himself to his feet with a pained grunt, got a drink of water, and then curled up to go back to sleep.

* * * *

Early the next morning, lights coming on and the anxious sounds of dogs barking awoke him. He wished he could understand them but the movie bullshit about shifters understanding what dogs said was just that—bullshit.

They still sounded like dogs.

Ain stared as three women and two men walked into the kennel area and started their morning routine. Looked like a pretty large shelter, wherever it was.

He stared up at the cards clipped to his gate. He couldn't read them, they faced the wrong way. He looked across the aisle, to where a beagle, a cocker mix, and a young Lab shared a run. Their cards he could read. At the top, the shelter's logo.

Roanoke Animal Rescue League.

Roanoke?

Fuck.

He groaned.

One of the women stopped in front of his run and looked at him. "Hey, boy. You okay?"

He looked at her and she reached a finger through the gate, scratched his head.

No. I'm not okay. I'm sooo fucking not okay it's not even funny.

Another woman walked up. "How is he?"

"I don't know. I'll get him out for a walk later and see how he's doing. He might not need any more pain meds. Are we getting any more from Florida?"

"Not from DeSoto County," the second woman said.

What the fuck?

"I hope they don't get whacked like Charley. That was a mess. My brother lives down there, near Orlando. He said they might evacuate up to Tallahassee."

What?

The woman stood and both walked away, talking.

No! What's going on?

He stared at another run across the aisle from his, and saw the cage card looked different. DeSoto County Animal Control. In black marker, someone had written on the card HURRICANE EVAC, HOLD FOR RETURN/RECLAIM.

He closed his eyes. *Oh, no.*

* * * *

The first rain bands would come through that night. The weather would really deteriorate by noon the next day. The boys put Elain in one of the guest rooms, the other two men at the far end of the house.

Once she felt sure the coast was clear she opened her door and two black dogs raced in. She closed and locked her door behind them. Brodey and Cail immediately shifted and sandwiched her between them.

"Jesus, babe!" Cail whispered, kissing her, holding her tightly. "I missed you so much!"

Brodey pressed into her from behind. "Dammit, it's good to have you home!"

Home. It *felt* good to be home.

Who was she kidding? She'd been miserable away from her boys. And worrying about Ain, the last thing she wanted to think about was her job.

With all three of them exhausted, they curled in bed together and she immediately fell into the first good sleep she'd had in days, comfortably sandwiched between her two men.

Two of her men.

She again wondered where and how Ain was.

When they got him back, she would give him a big fat honking piece of her mind.

Then she'd hug him and tell him she loved him.

The next day, they had to run into Arcadia again for another update from county officials, file a story, and get a live shot. Back to the ranch around noon. Wind gusts buffeted the van as they drove. The rain started as they pulled into the yard and they had to make a dash for the house. The men would move the van into the barn shortly.

Elain felt like pacing the house. She wanted to go to the bedroom—her bedroom, her real bedroom where she would normally sleep with her men—and curl up and cry.

She couldn't.

Cail caught her eye and winked. *"It's the storm. Barometer's dropping. It'll make you feel crazy,"* he silently thought to her.

Maybe that was the answer to her weird mood swings.

After they ate lunch, Carl went out with Brodey and Cail to move the news truck. Bill sat across from her in the living room. "Those guys really like you."

She fought her blush. "What are you talking about?" She hid her left hand. He apparently hadn't noticed her ring yet, hadn't commented on it.

He laughed. "They can't keep their eyes off you. I imagine there's gonna be some brotherly fighting for who gets to ask you out."

She didn't want to have this conversation. "Drop it, Bill."

"Where's Aindreas Lyall, anyway?"

"I think they said he's out handling stuff."

"Funny we haven't seen him around."

"Not my business."

He sat back and studied her. "There's something weird going on around here."

"What are you talking about?" She hoped she kept the anxious edge out of her voice.

"Those brothers. It's...I can't put my finger on it." He leaned in and dropped his voice. "Maybe they'll all ask you out. Lucky girl."

Now she knew he was busting her chops. Relieved, she pretended to be disgusted. "Bill, get your mind out of the gutter. Subject closed."

The wind howled outside the house. The other three returned and she had to fight not to get up, walk over, and kiss her two men.

She glanced at Bill and noticed he grinned at her.

* * * *

Ain tried to listen, to catch any bit of information he could. Someone turned on a radio, a local jazz station. Ain kept his ears peeled for newsbreaks.

Finally, at noon, his answer came. "Hurricane Natalia is bearing down on the Florida Gulf coast, nearly the same area ravaged by

Hurricane Charley a few years ago…"

Horrified, Ain listened to the story. If he could just get loose.

Then what? He would be a naked guy running around in Roanoke with no wallet, no ID.

And it wasn't like Brodey or Cail could come get him.

Did they find Elain? Was she safe?

He laid his head on his paws and whined.

* * * *

They got a few shots of the wind and weather from the front porch. Still too windy to transmit, and they couldn't bring the truck out of the barn to raise the dish, but Elain's laptop aircard received a signal so they could check the radar. The storm veered slightly to the south as it made landfall, putting them on the weaker side.

Brodey and Cail watched the screen over her shoulders. "That's good. We'll get Cat 2 gusts, but looks like only Cat 1 winds," Cail said. He looked at Brodey. "I think we dodged a bullet."

"What do you do after the storm?" she asked.

"Check the stock first, the barns, run the outer fence line with a vehicle and make emergency repairs to keep cattle from getting loose. If any have broke out, we look for them. Then we check the interior fences, make repairs, make sure the well pumps are working to keep the troughs filled. Things like that."

"What do you do with injured stock?"

Cail looked grim. "Depends on how badly. If they're severely injured, we put them down immediately. If it's minor, we get the vet out here to treat them if we can't handle it ourselves. A lot of them get lacerations from debris. Sometimes it's just minor and we can get by hosing them down with antiseptic. They'll be really stressed, so unless there's danger, we'll let them stay where they are for a day or so to calm down. We'll open up the calf barn, let them loose but not run them out. Once they settle, we'll cut them again and move them to their pastures after we check them out."

"How many did you lose after Charley?"

Brodey shook his head. "That was bad, man. Thirty died in the storm. Had to put down another fifty. Another forty injured, but the vet treated them. Nearly all of them had some sort of minor injury. That's why we built the reinforced barn, to at least get the most vulnerable ones to some sort of safety. Normally you don't put cattle in a barn for a storm, but we had this one specially made. Cost us over two million. It's like a bunker, with reinforced earthen and concrete berm walls and a roof rated up to Cat 4. It's not like we can drive the cattle across the state out of the way. They just have to hunker down and weather the storm. We dug windbreaks in the north pasture because it's the highest, no flooding, lots of cypress trees to act as natural windbreaks, too. All we can do is pray."

By that night, Elain felt like she'd crawl out of her skin. Between Ain missing, the storm and not being able to curl up with her men, she was a nervous wreck. Brodey and Cail both tried to mentally reassure her. She still felt upset. She went to bed and a little after eleven o'clock heard a soft scratching on the door. When she opened it, Cail and Brodey walked in.

They shifted and held her as she cried.

"I'm sorry," she apologized. "I can't do this. I'm so worried about him! What if he's hurt?"

"He's okay," Brodey reassured her. "I'm sure he is. He's tough."

She looked at Cail. "I'm going to quit. I can't stand this. I thought I could, I thought I wanted to work. I love you guys and I don't want to be away from you. I want him back. I'm still pissed at him, but I love him."

"Babe, don't make a rash decision. We told you, if you want to work, go ahead. We'll figure something out."

She shook her head. "No. I'm quitting. I can't do this. I hate feeling like this. I don't want to do this, I want to be with you guys."

He hugged her to him, Brodey pressing close behind. "Whatever you want," Brodey reassured her, "it's what we'll do."

They moved to the bed and held her. "How are we going to find him?" she said with a sniffle.

"I don't know, sweetie," Cail said. "Frankly, we can't worry about that until after we see what kind of damage we've got to deal with here. He's going to have to fend for himself."

* * * *

Ain slowly limped out of his run as one of the shelter techs led him outside. He could barely walk, he hurt so badly. Jesus, he'd fucked up big time.

From the news updates on the radio, the storm wouldn't be as bad as Charley. Heap the guilt on, he should have been at the ranch overseeing things.

How would they ever track him down in Roanoke?

He didn't want to live without Elain. He couldn't face his brothers now, after letting them down. What could he do?

He glanced at the woman holding his leash as an idea formed. Maybe he could finish this once and for all.

Ain looked at her, raised his hackles, and let out a low, deep growl.

Chapter Eight

Sunshine greeted Elain the next morning as she drank her first cup of coffee. Brodey and Cail had headed out at dawn to check the stock. She would follow soon after with Bill and Carl.

She had things to do, stories to file.

A job to quit.

She forced herself through the morning. Reluctantly, she rode back to Arcadia with Bill and Carl to get follow-up stories. She'd had to pack her things and bring them, because it would be too hard to explain why she didn't when they were returning to Venice that afternoon.

Aside from downed limbs and a few hanging power lines, the area didn't look any worse for wear. They truly had dodged a bullet.

Last stop, follow up with Animal Control. They arrived a little after ten o'clock. Elain talked with the shelter director and spread out the sheaf of fliers with pictures, descriptions, and information on the animals they'd shipped out to other shelters so Bill could get a shot of them.

"We finally had time to get these printed up," he explained. "We were too busy with storm prep to do it earlier."

Elain was about to turn from the counter when one caught her eye. *Stray, HBC, Male U/A, Black, Grey Eyes, Shep/Wolf Hybrid.*

She snatched the paper from the counter. Lying on his side with an IV in his front leg, but it was Ain, she'd bet her life on it. She turned to the shelter manager. "What does this mean? HBC? U/A?"

The manager took the paper. "Oh, he's the one hit by a car. U/A—Unaltered. Male, not neutered."

Elain forced the words out. "Hit by a car?"

He nodded. "Yeah, an old couple in one of those tiny cars hit him. Thank God he wasn't badly hurt, they were poking along pretty slow. We shipped him out to Roanoke the other day. Just before you got here, as a matter of fact. That was the first trailer load we transported."

Bill caught her arm as she swayed on her feet. "Jesus, Elain, are you okay?"

"No." She snatched the paper back from the shelter manager. "Where is he right now? He's in Roanoke? *Virginia*?"

"Yeah. Why? Do you know him?"

"He's one of the...Lyall brothers' dogs. He went missing before the storm. He's...he's a stock dog, working dog. Cattle."

Bill looked at the paper. "Hell, yeah, he does look like those other two, doesn't he?"

The shelter manager smiled. "Oh, well that's great! I'll call Roanoke right now and tell them to make sure they hold him." He walked to his office. When he returned a moment later, his face looked decidedly grimmer than when he'd left.

"What's wrong?" Elain fought the urge to scream the words.

"He...um, he bit a shelter worker yesterday. He's acting very aggressive. They've tagged him for euthanasia as a vicious dog after his quarantine period is up. They said they can't get near him."

Elain ran outside. With shaking hands she called Brodey, then Cail. Both went straight to voicemail.

She returned to the front desk and grabbed the paper, shook it in the manager's face. "What do I need to claim him?"

"What? I doubt they'll let you—"

Elain strangled back the sudden rage that welled up inside her. "*What* do I need to claim him? They *can't* put him down!" *He's my mate!* "He's...I can't get hold of the Lyall brothers, but I know he's their dog. He's a very valuable dog, he's current on his vaccinations, and he's not vicious!" *He's just heartbroken.*

"This is very irregular."

She stared him down. "*Give* me paperwork," she growled, surprised again at the emotion in her voice. "*Call* the shelter in Roanoke, tell them I'll be there as soon as I can get a flight out."

Bill touched her arm. "Um, Elain? We have film to shoot."

She wheeled around and fought the urge to bare her teeth at him. "I *won't* let them put him down! That's…his name's Alpha. He's one of their dogs. I know he's had all his shots, he's up to date."

Bill backed up a step, held his hands up in front of him. "Whoa, girl. Okay. Whatever."

The shelter manager gave her his card, wrote his personal cell and home numbers on it, and gave her release paperwork from their shelter. "Considering he's bitten someone, I doubt they'll let you walk out of there with him. That releases him from our custody on this end, have them call me personally with any questions. Normally I wouldn't do stuff like this. There are procedures we're supposed to follow, you know."

"Thank you."

Elain dragged Bill and Carl back to the truck and fought her emotions all the way to the station. She didn't even bother going inside, just threw her things into her car and immediately headed for Tampa International Airport. So much for her job.

Hell, this is getting real *fucking old.*

She rummaged through her stuff, jammed a few things into her overnight bag, and found a flight leaving in forty minutes for Richmond. It wouldn't get her there before the shelter closed. She wasn't picky.

On the ground in Virginia, she rented a car and drove to Roanoke, arrived at the shelter a little after ten that night.

No one there, the gate was locked.

She found an open restaurant and used the bathroom, freshened up, and forced herself to eat. Her phone was dead, she'd forgotten to charge it and didn't have the charger with her.

She'd forgotten it at home.

At the ranch.

She stopped by a Wal-Mart that was open all night and bought a couple of things. A little after midnight, Elain parked outside the shelter, locked her car doors, and tipped back the driver seat to wait.

* * * *

The first workers arrived around six-thirty the next morning. Elain grabbed her new tote bag and the paperwork and approached them, explained the situation.

The woman looked dubious. "Lady, that dog is freaking vicious. We can't get near close to him now. He just suddenly went nuts. They're not going to let you anywhere near him."

Elain felt near tears again. "Please! I *know* him. Look, I've got all his paperwork. Animal Control in Arcadia released him, said I can take him. He's had his shots, he doesn't need to be quarantined. I flew up here from Florida to get him. *Please!*"

"The shelter manager doesn't get in for another hour yet. He's got to be the one to make the call." She sighed. "It won't hurt to let you get a look at him, I suppose, just to confirm he's the same dog." She waved Elain through the gate and led her inside the building.

* * * *

Ain waited. He heard the door unlock, the lights came on. He felt bad about biting the woman, hoped he didn't hurt her, only wanted to scare her. He didn't think he broke the skin. His vicious snarling and growling and barking went a long way to instilling fear in them.

This must be what it feels like being on death row.

He closed his eyes and waited. They'd moved him to a securely locked section, in one of several runs reserved for quarantined dogs.

Vicious dogs.

He'd have to keep the act up until they finally put him down.

When the first woman came in, Ain lifted his head and snarled.

"Yeah, same to you, asshole," she muttered as she unlocked his gate. She quickly slid a bowl of food inside the door before slamming it shut again.

When she left, Ain dropped his head to his paws. The food sucked. *How did dogs stand this shit?*

He wouldn't eat it. It didn't matter, he'd hopefully be dead in a couple of days anyway. He closed his eyes and thought about Elain. He missed her, missed his brothers. If he thought about her hard enough, he could almost smell her.

The outer gate opened again, footsteps approached, two people.

He growled.

Leave me alone.

A woman's voice. "Good luck. I'm telling you, no one can get near him."

He growled louder, preparing to launch into a full snarl. He lifted his head and opened his eyes, the growl dying in his throat.

Elain smiled at him. "Do you know how worried we've been about you, asshole?"

* * * *

Elain would have laughed at Ain's shocked expression if she wasn't so fricking relieved to find him and worried about getting him out the shelter's front door. She had a pair of shorts, a T-shirt, and flip-flops in his size stashed in the tote bag on her shoulder, but she'd also spotted the video cameras in the shelter. If she couldn't get Alpha the dog out, she thought she might be able to get Ain out on two legs if she could get him somewhere he could shift without being seen.

He stared at her in apparent shock while she knelt in front of the run.

"Don't stick your hand in there, ma'am," the shelter worker

warned. "I'm telling, you, he's—"

Ain leaped to his feet despite the pain it caused and rushed the gate. He jammed his nose against it trying to lick Elain, happily whining, wagging his tail.

"Jesus!" the shelter worker said. "I thought he was going to eat you!"

Elain laughed. "No, he's just stressed out. He's a working dog, not a pet. He's normally herding thousand-pound cows. He's not a normal dog and he's not used to being in a kennel. I'm telling you, he's not a vicious dog." She stood and opened the run, stepped inside with him, knelt down again.

She wrapped her arms around him and buried her face against his fur.

"You are, however, a fucking asshole."

"I know, babe! I'm so sorry! I'm so, so sorry! Oh Goddess, I'm so sorry! I love you so much!"

She grabbed his face in her hands and looked into his eyes. *"No more bullshit edicts?"*

"I promise."

"Teach me what I need to know, I promise I'll try to learn. But please, no edicts unless it's shifter shit. You do not have to force me to stay with you, got it?"

"I promise! Oh, Goddess, I promise! Anything!"

She hugged him again, deeply inhaling his scent. "I love you," she whispered in his ear. "I love you so much. I thought we'd lost you."

He whined.

It took a lot of begging, pleading, and demonstration that Ain was definitely not a vicious dog to finally convince the shelter manager to release him to Elain two hours later. The only thing in Ain's favor was that the overcrowded shelter didn't want to euthanize him.

Ain walked up to the woman he'd bit. He whined and licked her hand. Fortunately he hadn't injured her. She finally laughed and also asked the shelter manager to release him.

With a kennel lead looped around Ain's neck, Elain signed paperwork and led him out of the shelter, opened the back door of her rental car for him. "In, asshole," she said.

Still very sore, he carefully climbed in with a pained grunt and lay down on the seat.

She slid behind the wheel and looked over the seat at him. "I slept in the freaking car last night. I've got to call Brodey and Cail, and my job is probably moot at this point because I basically walked off to come get you when I found out what happened. You are in so much fucking trouble, buddy."

He whined.

Elain found a hotel, checked in, didn't mention her "dog" but said her fiancé was with her. She left Ain in the car, drove them around the corner to a fast food restaurant and went through drive-thru, then returned to the hotel.

She opened the back door for him, grabbed her bag and purse and the food, unlocked the room door and put their things inside. Ain carefully climbed out of the car with her help and limped into the room. She followed him inside and locked the door behind her after putting out the Do Not Disturb sign.

He put his front paws up on the bed and shifted.

"Oh, Goddess, I fucking hurt!" he groaned.

She wanted to stay mad but the massive swaths of black and blue along his torso and thigh short-circuited that emotion.

"Holy shit!" She raced to his side and gently helped him onto the bed. An awful odor assaulted her nose. "Oh, sweetie, no offense, you really stink. You smelled better as a dog."

Several days of stubble shadowed his cheeks. He harshly laughed. "Yeah, I imagine. Give me a minute to catch my breath and help me into the shower, please?"

She started the shower, got the water warming, then stripped and helped him inside. He was in too much pain to do anything except lean against the wall while she carefully swabbed him clean and shaved him. They finished and she helped him dry off and walk back to the bed where he sat with a pained grunt.

She handed him his food. "Eat. Then we need to call the others."

He wouldn't look at her. "I'm sorry, Elain. I mean it."

She knelt in front of him. "Look at me."

He finally did, his grey eyes full of sadness.

"You don't need to order me to stay with you and not work and all that shit. But when you tell me you're going to do one thing, and I find out you fucked with my mind, that hurts. And it pisses me off. Why should I trust anything you tell me?"

"I'm sorry. You're right."

She gently patted his leg. "Eat."

She called the ranch from the room phone. When they finally reached Brodey, he was first upset she'd left again without saying anything, then happy she'd found Ain.

"Let me speak to Mr. Prime Asshole."

"Go easy on him, he's had a rough few days."

"Fuck that. I've got a bone to pick with him, babe."

She handed over the phone and watched as Ain closed his eyes and listened to Brodey rant and rave for five minutes. He couldn't get a word in edgewise.

When Brodey finished, she heard him yell, "And what do you say to all of that, you goddamned asshole?"

"That you're right, and I'm sorry."

Stunned silence from the phone.

"You still there, Brod?" Ain asked.

"Sorry?"

"Yeah. I acted like an asshole. I brought this all on myself. You're right."

"Let me talk to Elain." Aindreas handed the phone over and with a pained groan stretched out on the bed.

"Yeah?"

"Is he okay? Conk on the head?"

"Yes to both. I'll catch up when we get home."

"When?"

"I don't know yet. I have to sleep, and he's in too much pain to move right now. I'll let you know."

"Thanks."

She hung up and carefully climbed into bed next to him. "You've got a lot of sucking up to do, mister."

"Yeah. No arguments from me."

Elain gently laced her fingers through his. "How did you get hit by a car?"

He didn't answer.

"You were trying to kill yourself, weren't you?"

He finally nodded.

"And that's why you bit the shelter worker? You thought they'd put you down?"

He nodded again.

"I'm not a complicated woman. I want to be able to trust the man—men—I'm spending the rest of my life with. That's all."

He carefully rolled over and nuzzled his face against her shoulder. "I'm sorry."

"How long until you can travel, do you think?"

"I don't have ID. I can't fly."

"Shit." She climbed out of bed, got Brodey on the phone again, and he agreed to overnight her phone charger and Ain's wallet to the hotel. She climbed back into bed.

"Okay, so you've got at least twenty-four hours alone with me. First, let's sleep. When we wake up, I'll go get us lunch and we'll get you some real clothes and talk."

He closed his eyes. "Sounds good to me."

* * * *

The bruises actually looked better when they awoke later that afternoon. He studied his wounds in the mirror. "I bet they looked even worse the other day," he said.

"I thought you said you heal faster than a normal human?"

"We do. All I had were some cracked ribs and a concussion. Any normal dog would have probably nearly died. I can finally breathe without pain now."

She winced. "You took a lickin', that's for sure."

"We can try for a flight out tomorrow evening if there is one and my wallet gets here in time."

She sat on the bed and stared at him. He turned. "What?"

She shrugged. "Maybe you and I need this alone time. Hash some shit out. Brodey and Cail are going to ream you a new one when we get home." She noticed he hadn't said a word about her swearing.

"Yeah."

She stood and walked over to him, gently put her arms around him. "If I even still have a job, I'm going to tell them that I'm quitting."

"Babe, you don't need to—"

"Shh. Let me say this. You were right, okay? I hated being away from you guys. I was so pissed and upset when I left for Spokane, I couldn't think straight. When Brodey showed up and found me, I wanted him to bring me home."

She looked into his eyes. "Yes, it feels like home, being with you guys. I admit it. I don't know what I want to do but I can't work for the station. That's two hours a day driving around that I could be with you guys. And you and Brodey are right that even if I'm not on-air, it's not safe for us to be together if I'm working there."

He rested his chin on top of her head. "I've managed to fuck this up all the way around, haven't I?"

"Well, the fastest way to stop doing that is quit thinking there are things you should be doing, and just go by what we need to do for the four of us, got it?"

"Yeah."

"Spend time with me. Talk to me. Teach me. If you have to edict me for some reason, as soon as it's safe, explain why and let me talk with you about it. It won't piss me off as much. I don't want to do anything to screw things up around other shifters. Do not edict me just to shut me up or to have sex or whatever."

"I'd never do that!"

"See, that's my point. How do I know? That's what scared me after that little stunt you pulled. You can force me to do things and frankly, it freaks me out."

"I'm sorry," he softly said.

He felt okay enough to ride in the car. Elain bought him a pair of jeans, a shirt, and real shoes. Then they stopped for lunch. When they returned to the room, Ain stripped and she noticed one of the bruises on his hip had almost nearly faded.

"Look there." She gently touched the spot. "It's healing."

He nodded. "Yeah, it should go pretty fast now." She noticed he wasn't limping as badly either.

They watched TV in bed. Elain admitted the feel of Ain's arms around her was pretty nice after so many days away from him.

She slid his hand from where it rested around her waist up to her breast.

He kissed the back of her neck. "Is that a hint?"

"Yeah. If you're up to it."

He stiffened against her ass in response. "Oh, yeah. I'm up to it." He trailed his lips down to her shoulder. "I don't think I deserve it though."

"Yeah, you're in the doghouse, buddy."

He laughed. "First I need to get back in your good graces, then I need to suck up to Brodey and Cail."

She snorted. "No kidding. They'll have your hide, Prime or not, when you get home."

"How much storm damage? Did we lose any cattle?"

"I don't know. It wasn't as bad as they first thought it would be.

Arcadia was mostly in one piece when we drove through." She turned over and glared at him. "I left before I could find out. I had to fly up here and rescue a stray mutt."

He rolled on top of her. "Point made." He pressed his lips to hers and her next irritated, snarky comment flew out of her head at the taste and feel of him against her.

When he lifted his head and broke their kiss, she asked, "Is this what a drug addict feels like when they get their next hit?"

He smiled. "Drug addict?"

"Yeah." She ran her hands down his firm back. "I'm still mad at you, and here I am, ready to jump you."

He kissed her again. "Yeah?"

"Yeah," she breathlessly answered. "You hurt my feelings. You pissed me off. To top it all off, you scared the crap out of me by disappearing."

He nuzzled the base of her throat, his tongue and lips hot against her skin. "I'll spend the rest of my life apologizing."

She closed her eyes and enjoyed what he did to her. "Maybe only the next couple of weeks. *If* you don't stop doing that."

His deep chuckle stirred something inside her. He worked his way lower and lifted her shirt, kissed her belly. "How about this?"

"Mmm. Maybe. Does this make me a slut for being so easy?"

He sat up, faster than she could follow the movement, and grabbed her wrists. "Stop." His grip was firm, but not painful. "Don't ever say that about yourself."

Sudden anger welled up in her, unstoppable. "Well isn't what this all boils down to? It's like I've lost my brain and what little sanity I had since I met the three of you! I had a fucking—FUCKING career, a life! Don't get me wrong, you three are worth it, but now it's like I've got no will of my own..." She broke down sobbing. "And now I've got these stupid mood swings! It's all your fault!"

She took a swing at him but he wrapped his arms around her and held her to him, kissing the top of her head, trying to soothe her.

"Sweetie, this is more than conscious thought or feeling. This is Fate. Forces beyond us brought us all together. Believe me, we're just as crazy about you as you are about us. Maybe more. We don't think of you like that at all. We think you're the perfect woman for us, the *only* woman for us. We were meant to find and love you."

She sniffled against his chest. "I've lost my mind."

He covered her face with kisses. "We love you. You don't understand, we haven't had time to teach you anything yet." He gently touched her chin and made her look at him. "We are bound by the Code of the Ancients. When we find our One, we are sworn to protect them, love them, and make them happy. For the rest of our lives together, we will do whatever it takes to make you happy and take care of you."

"It would make me happy to work."

He hugged her tighter. "I know. Maybe we can find something else you can do that you'd enjoy that's closer to home."

"I worked so hard to get on the air."

"I'm sorry."

"I'm sick of you apologizing."

He bit back the urge to apologize again. Instead, he sighed. "I told you, if you want to work, we'll figure something out."

"I can't. Brodey was right. If I work at the station then I can't be open with you guys. It could bring attention. And I don't want to be away from you guys that much."

He feathered his lips across her forehead. "We can sell the ranch," he softly said.

"What?"

"If you're really that miserable, we can sell the ranch and we'll move to Venice. We'll need to get a bigger house though, find someplace private, without neighbors close by."

"You'd do that for me?"

"If it's what would make you happy."

But that wouldn't make her boys happy, and she knew it. They would only be doing it for her. They'd been there for over fifty years—that was still hard to wrap her brain around—and she knew from her talks with Brodey that they loved having the woods to run in, loved working with the cattle.

"No."

His eyebrows arched in surprise. She explained. "What would really make me happy is to have some time to chill out, the four of us, to figure out what the hell is normal. Time so you guys can teach me whatever dog rules there are so I don't screw up, and time to get to know each other. Normal. I want peace and calm."

He nodded.

She sighed and snuggled closer. "I'm a freak."

"No, you're not."

"I am! I mean, let's face it, look at how I pant over the three of you!"

He rolled on top of her again. "Don't make me edict you to not worry about this." His tone and playful smile belied his words.

"Maybe this is one time I'd let you get away with that."

He kissed the tip of her nose. "Maybe you could write erotic fiction based on our life. Don't those kinds of books make a lot of money?"

She laughed. "Only you would think of that."

"No, I'm sure Brodey would. He's the original horn dog." He lifted her shirt again, this time up and over her head. When he spoke, his voice sounded quiet. "I want to make you happy, Elain. I want to spend my life loving you."

"Why were you trying to kill yourself?"

He wouldn't meet her eyes. She caught his chin and made him look at her. "Brodey said something about you guys cannot lie to each other, and now you can't lie to me since we're mated."

"It would have broken your bond to me. I wanted you to be happy."

"If I make you promise something, you're bound by that?"

He nodded.

"Promise me you won't ever do something so freaking stupid like that again."

"I promise."

She pulled him to her and kissed him, wrapped her arms around him. This time she let her passion take over and kick her stubborn mind out of control. Her body responded to his touch, to the heat in his hands as they skimmed down her body.

She lifted her hips when he unfastened her shorts, so he could slide them down her legs, along with her panties. Then he settled his mouth over her mound and gently flicked her clit.

She moaned.

He trailed kisses along her inner thighs. "I'm so sorry, babe."

"I told you to quit apologizing."

He chuckled and laved her clit with his tongue again, drawing a deep, satisfied hiss from her. "That's more like it," she said.

Ain wrapped his arms around her thighs, his hands firmly holding her to him. It didn't take him long to bring her over. His tongue mercilessly worked her clit until she finally cried out and bucked her hips against him.

He slipped inside her and rolled to his side, slowly fucking her. She hooked her leg around his, one hand slipping around his hip, her fingers digging into his ass.

He nuzzled the base of her throat. "How about I make a deal with you? No bullshit. You give us six months, do things my way."

She froze and leaned back to look at him. "Whoa. What do you mean your way?"

"Hear me out."

She relaxed against him. "Go ahead."

He resumed his slow strokes. "You give us six months. You said you wanted peace and quiet. Normalcy. You give us those six months, we can teach you, let you mentally decompress. Then, if at the end of six months, if you really want to go back to work, you can. And I won't stop you or let Brod or Cail stop you."

"Really?"

"Yeah."

She studied him. "Even in front of the camera?"

He frowned. "I would prefer you didn't."

She smiled. "I won't. I just wanted to see what you'd say." She ground her hips against his and enjoyed the feel of his thick cock sliding inside her. "Six months. You didn't answer my question about what you meant by your way."

"I already told you I won't edict you to force you to stay."

"What's the catch? You try to get me pregnant?"

He smiled and kissed her, long and deeply. "No. I already told you I don't want that yet. One day, yes. We spent too many years trying to find you to jump right into midnight feedings and dirty diapers. The three of us are looking forward to a lot of play time with you first."

"I think you really mean that. But don't we need to think about that sooner than later?"

"Why?"

"Hello, tick tock. Biological clock."

He grinned and rolled on top of her again. "Babe, that's all part of the package. You just got a huge extension on that."

"Years?"

"Decades, at the very least." He kissed her again, thrust inside her. "I think I'm going to need quite a few of those years to fully earn your trust back." He still felt her reluctance, her anger.

Her fear.

"You're counting on me not wanting to go back to work at the end of six months, aren't you?"

"We're going to show you what being treated like a princess is really like." He kissed her again. "We're going to spoil you rotten." He blazed a trail of kisses down her neck to her right breast, gently flicked her nipple with his tongue. "We're going to do any and everything within our power to do to make and keep you happy." He kissed across her chest to her other breast, teased that nipple into a hard peak. "We're going to show you how much we love you."

He kissed her again. "You can make the decision whether you really want to go back to work or not. You don't ever have to work again, if you don't want to. Or, you could even go back to college if you wanted something to do."

Between the feel of him inside her and what his incredibly addictive mouth did to her body, she could barely think. She met his gaze. "Okay," she whispered. "No games?"

"No games, babe."

She grabbed his head, tangled her fingers in his hair, and crushed her lips to his. "Any and everything?"

He nodded, smiled. "We've got a big bank account."

She laughed. "Show me how much you love me, big guy."

His release pounded through him. He grabbed her hips and thrust, burying himself deep inside her as he came, moaning her name. Then he gathered her into his arms and rolled to his side again and held her. "I love you so much, Elain."

She snuggled tightly against him. "I'm holding you to that promise."

"No problem."

Chapter Nine

Elain didn't feel like going out to eat so she ordered them a pizza. After they finished eating, she called the ranch collect on the room phone and talked with Cail and Brodey. The two brothers spoke civilly to Ain this time. He learned with no small measure of relief that the ranch sustained only minor damage and no cattle were lost or severely injured.

Elain limited his time on the phone, wanted him to rest. He felt much better, nearly half the original bruises already healed, the rest fading out to ugly shades of brownish green that she suspected would be mostly gone by the next afternoon. She talked to Brodey, then Cail, before they turned in for the night.

The next morning, they took a long, steamy shower, ended up back in bed, then back in the shower again. Elain was surprised to see Ain's bruises had nearly completely healed, even faster than she imagined he would be.

"I told you, it goes fast. Bruises usually heal pretty quickly."

Her fingers traced his flesh, which had been previously covered in deep purple and now looked perfectly normal. "Will I be able to do that?"

He scooped her into his arms again. "Babe, I don't want to find out how well you can heal. I'd kill anyone who tried to hurt you. But yes, mates usually gain some ability to heal faster."

By the time they returned to the hotel from their long, late breakfast, a package waited for them at the front desk. Her cell charger and Ain's wallet.

He flipped through it, slipped it into his jeans. "Now I can start paying for stuff again."

The way he said it made her insides flutter in a good way. "What, my money's not any good?"

His eyes burned into hers. "What part of spoiled rotten princess don't you understand, babe?"

She smiled. "I've never been spoiled rotten before."

When he smiled, it transformed his serious stare into a sweet, sultry look that screamed "fuck me!"

"Get used to it." He leaned in closer so the hotel desk clerk couldn't hear him, and he whispered in her ear, "You've got three guys who are going to spoil you rotten."

She shivered in a pleasant way.

"You could have said that mentally."

He smiled. With a feather-light touch he brushed his fingers up her arm, triggering yet another shiver from her. *"It wouldn't have been as effective."*

"Tease," she whispered.

His eyes crinkled in amusement. "Not me." He pressed his lips to the spot behind her ear that he'd figured out melted her reserve. *"Let's go back to the room and I'll show you how much of a tease I'm not while your phone charges."*

She gasped.

Back at the room, she slammed the door shut behind them, flipped the deadbolt, and leaped at him. He caught her, his lips hungrily devouring hers as they fell to the bed. She landed on top of him.

"Why do you do this to me?" Elain asked. "I feel like I've got no self-control around you." She ripped her shirt off and flung it to the floor.

He smiled. "Sort of that whole fated to be together thing I keep telling you about." He rolled her over, pinning her to the bed, his fingers lacing through hers. He tormented her by teasing her nipples with his lips. "If I was an asshole, I'd edict you into staying naked all the time so I could fuck you whenever I wanted. I can't keep my hands off you."

"You wouldn't!" She had to admit the thought made her wet.

"No, I wouldn't." He lifted his head, met her gaze, then smiled. "Why? Do you want me to?" He playfully arched an eyebrow, questioning her.

"Who says you have to edict me?" She tried to kiss him again. He stayed tortuously out of reach.

He grinned and released her hands. She helped him unfasten and slide her shorts off her hips. When he buried his face between her legs, she moaned. He didn't speak again until he made her come. He shucked his pants and rolled her over onto her stomach. When he pulled her to her knees, she froze.

He read her body. "No," he softly said, trailing kisses down her spine. "Not that. I meant it when I said never again if you don't want it. We had to do that for the Ceremony."

He waited until she relaxed to slide inside her wet heat. Then he folded his body around her. With his arms wrapped around her, he slowly thrust, enjoying the feel of her. He feathered kisses along the nape of her neck and nuzzled the mark he'd placed on the back of her right shoulder during their marking Ceremony. He felt her shiver in his arms as he gently scraped his teeth along the mark.

Ain pulled her into a sitting position against his chest and slid one hand between her legs. "Can you give me another one?"

Her head lolled against his shoulder. "I...don't know."

With a gentle nip to her neck, he stroked her clit. "Try."

She shivered again, in the way he knew meant she was close to the edge. He felt her muscles clench around him. He kept his other arm tightly around her, holding her against him as he mercilessly teased her closer to release.

"Do it, baby," he whispered against her neck. "I want to feel you squeeze my cock."

Then she shuddered, crying out as her climax hit. He waited a moment before pushing her back down to the bed. He grabbed her hips and thrust, finishing with her. They collapsed to the bed and he held her tightly, still inside her.

They were both dozing when her cell phone rang. He was closer, and he groaned with irritation when he saw it was Brodey.

He unplugged it from the charger and answered it. "What?"

"Don't you what me, Prime Asshole. When's your flight?"

Elain tried to reach for the phone but he captured her hand, brought it to his lips and kissed it. "We haven't made the reservations yet."

"What the fuck? Your shit got there over an hour ago. I got the delivery confirmation email."

She made another grab for the phone. Ain leaned over and kissed her, then made a soft, low warning growl in the back of his throat. "We got distracted."

"Oh, fuck me, that's just great. We're here busting our asses and you're getting laid."

Ain knew she could hear Brodey over the phone because of the way she smiled at Brodey's comment. "We'll go to the airport after a while."

"Fuck that shit. You bring her home. Now."

He sat up. "*What* did you just say to me?"

"You heard me. You don't get to pull Prime bullshit, not after the last couple of days and what you put us all through."

He started to reply when he felt Elain's hand grab his crotch, and not in a gentle, playful way. She held her other hand out, palm up, for the phone.

He started to say something when he looked into her eyes.

"Now, Ain."

He sighed. He did have this coming. He handed the phone over. She immediately released him and turned away, moving to the side of the bed. "Hey, sweetie."

"There you are. What the hell?"

"Where are you?"

"Um, Florida, babe."

She fought the urge to giggle. "Brod, honey, focus. Are you in the house, out in the field, where?"

"Oh. I'm out at the north barn. Why?"

"Where's Cail?"

"He's at the house."

"I'm going to hang up and call him there. I'll call you back when we've got the flight information."

That seemed to mollify him. "Okay. Is the Prime prick giving you any hassle?"

"It's under control, sweetie." She stood as she ended the call and walked out of Ain's reach. She was well aware of his eyes on her as she dialed Cail and waited for him to answer.

"Babe, are you on your way back yet?"

"No sweetie, I need you to look something up..."

Ain sat while she had Cail make them flight reservations. She found Ain's wallet and handed it to him. He rummaged through it and handed her a credit card to use. Cail got them onto a flight leaving at six that night, plenty of time for them to get back to the airport. Ten minutes later she hung up and called Brodey back. Another five minutes later, she put the phone on the charger and returned the card to Ain. Then she pushed him down on the bed and straddled him.

"Listen. You really pissed them off, buddy. And you hurt their feelings. Not to mention you scared the crap out of them. Do *not* get into it with them."

Ain's urge to re-establish his Prime status battled with what his heart and brain knew was right. "He had no right to talk to me like that."

She kissed the end of his nose and climbed off the bed again before he could entice her back into it. "Yes, he did. You acted like an assh—" She looked at him. "You were a real jerk."

He stared for a moment, then laughed. "Thank you."

"You don't go hauling off and spanking me if I swear, though.

That's just bullpucky."

He stood and hugged her. "You promised me six months of doing things my way."

"And you promised me a kinder, gentler Prime."

He grinned and scooped her into his arms, headed for the bathroom. "Let's grab one more shower and hit the road so we can go home. I've got some sucking up to do."

* * * *

Ain took the rental car keys and held the passenger door open for her after he loaded what little they had into the car.

Elain had to admit she liked that part, being treated like a princess.

She gave him directions to the airport and they had enough time for dinner at a restaurant there before making their way to the gate.

"You have to remember," she said, keeping her voice low, "I don't know you guys. Really. Yeah, I love you. But I don't know you, and you don't know me."

He reached for her hand across the table and laced his fingers through hers. "I love you. That's all I need to know."

"Most women would be under heavy sedation at this point, buddy. Give me brownie points for not running and screaming."

He smiled. "You recognized us the way we recognized you."

"This is way more than compatible pheromones."

"It's magic." He kissed her hand and winked.

Dammit, she wished he wouldn't do that. It made her want to drag him into bed.

Again.

Fortunately their food arrived. She glanced across the table as they ate. A thought struck her, and she grinned.

He noticed. "What?"

She sat back and crossed her arms, triumphant. "You'll do anything to make me happy?"

He froze, sensing a trap, his fork midway to his mouth. "Yeah?"

The smile nearly split her face in two. "Anything?"

He set his fork down. "Depends."

"Nope. You have to agree to it."

"That's not—"

She glared as a low, deep growl sounded in the back of her throat. It surprised her, but felt instinctive. Maybe that was another effect of their mating.

He arched an eyebrow at her. "I suggest you back down," he softly said, but the force behind his eyes contradicted his tone.

She narrowed her glance. "Well?"

"You tell me first. Then I'll tell you if I agree or not."

"It has nothing to do with me working."

He studied her. Finally he said, "Fine. What is it?"

"You have to speak Scottish for me."

He closed his eyes and groaned. "Babe, please, no."

"Brodey does it for me." That was a cheap shot and she knew it.

He rolled his eyes, but he gritted his teeth and lowered his voice. "And what would you have me say, lassie?" A perfect Scottish brogue rolled from his hunky lips.

She gulped, hard. Dammit he sounded yummy like that! "Just...talk like that," she gasped.

A playful smile filled his face. He would get his pound of flesh in retaliation for agreeing. "And what, exactly, are ye gonna do with me talkin' like this?"

She closed her eyes and took a deep breath. "You wanted to get back into my good graces. You keep talking like that and I'll be humping you in the airplane."

He sat back and took a sip of his iced tea. "Well, I wouldn't want ta be dissapointin' ye now, would I?"

Chapter Ten

Ain did manage to keep Elain from raping him on the airplane. Back at Tampa International, he took her car keys from her and carried their bags, held the passenger door open for her, all while still maintaining his brogue.

In the car she leaned over and kissed him, hard. "I know this is stupid, but I can't help it. I love the way you guys sound when you talk like that."

He dropped the brogue. "I can't talk like this all the time, sweetie."

"Why not? You grew up in Scotland."

"Because we've got an image to uphold. Everyone knows us in Arcadia. Around you, okay, sure." He gently stroked her cheek. "Besides, you don't want to get too used to it, get bored."

"You walk around in a kilt and talking like Braveheart, trust me, I won't get tired of it."

He laughed and started the car, returning to the brogue. "I suppose I can talk like that a wee bit more for ye."

She sighed in contentment.

* * * *

It was a little after midnight when they pulled into the yard. The front porch lights were on, casting some light. Brodey and Cail raced out the door to greet them when they heard the car.

The two brothers first surrounded her, hugging and kissing her. Then Brodey lunged around the car, tackling Ain as he got out. Elain screamed, but Cail grabbed her by the waist and held on tight.

"No, sweetie," he murmured in her ear. "Let them go at it. It'll be over in a minute."

Elain sobbed as they fought, rolling around in the grass, both landing vicious punches on each other, snarling and growling even though they weren't shifted.

"They're going to hurt each other!"

"No, they won't. You need to let them do it." His voice turned hard and cold. "Then it's my turn."

The brothers fought for over five minutes. Elain gasped when Brodey let out a pained yelp. Ain knelt over him, his hand on Brodey's throat.

Brodey held up a hand and Ain released him, stood, then turned to Cail.

Cail let out a growl. Before she could reach for him, he let go of her and launched himself over the hood of the car at Ain, tackling him. Elain tried to race after him but Brodey, who'd jumped up and out of the way, intercepted her. He had a split lip and would have a black eye in the morning.

"Don't do it, babe," he warned as she cried and tried to fight her way free. He wrapped his arms around her and pinned her arms to her side, holding her too tightly for her to break free.

"Stop it!" she screamed. "Cail, leave him alone!"

"It's okay," Brodey assured her. "It's normal."

The two men duked it out, Cail lasting longer than Brodey had, but not by much. When Ain pinned him, Cail raised his hand and Ain immediately released him and stood. Then he extended his hand to his brother and helped him off the ground.

Elain watched, amazed, as the two men hugged.

"You're a fucking asshole, Ain," Cail said, slapping him on the back. "You fucking owe me three goddamned days of sleep."

Ain looked worse than the other two men and he spit blood off to the side as he wiped at his lip. "Yeah, I know. I'm sorry."

Brodey finally released Elain, then he also hugged Ain. "Gonna kick your ass one of these days."

"Not any time soon."

Elain stood there, her heart pounding, her body shaking.

"What the fuck was that about?" she screamed at them.

The men turned to her. Ain smiled and gently pulled her to him. "It's okay, babe. I expected it. I deserved it. I'm sorry I didn't warn you. I kind of knew that would happen."

She jerked away from him and shoved Brodey, then Cail. "What the hell were you doing?"

Brodey caught her hands. "Honey, it's…" He looked at Cail. "Help me out here."

"It's a shifter thing. Pack order. We know damn well we aren't going to kick his ass, but he also needs to know how pissed we are."

Ain gently turned her to face him. In the deep shadows cast by the porch lights, she saw he also had a cut on his cheek. "It's okay," he said. "Seriously." He enveloped her in his arms, stroked her back. "You promised me six months to do things our way, remember?"

"You didn't say anything about beating the shit out of each other!" she sobbed.

He let that one go, probably because she was so upset. "We'll be healed up by lunch tomorrow. It's okay." He scooped her into his arms and carried her into the house while Brodey and Cail grabbed their things from the car.

He set her on their bed but in the bedroom light she gasped at how battered his face looked. He started to protest when she got up, but she growled at him.

"I need to clean that up." She started for the bathroom when Cail and Brodey appeared. "Sit on the bed so I can take care of you assholes, too," she snarled.

The men exchanged a glance, then sat without a word.

Ain watched her walk into the bathroom. "I think she's close to her period—"

"I heard that!" she yelled from the bathroom.

The men fell silent.

She returned a moment later with a first aid kit and swabbed their scrapes and cuts, used a butterfly bandage on Ain's cut, dabbed antiseptic ointment on their wounds. When she was satisfied, she stood back and looked at the three of them, crossed her arms.

"Do you morons do that a lot?"

The men shrugged. Brodey and Cail looked at Ain. "Not all the time," he explained. "Only when we get really pissed."

She jabbed her finger at them. "A little fu—freaking warning would have been nice! I don't want to see that sh-stuff." She ignored Ain's amused smile. "You guys have your rules? Well, here's one of mine if you really want to keep me happy. If you're going to do that, you take it outside, away from where I can see it."

"You can't get between us when we're fighting. You might get hurt," Ain said.

She glared at them. "How do you know I won't hurt one of *you*?"

The men exchanged an amused glance, obviously trying to hide their smiles. "I don't think you could hurt us, babe," Ain said. He stood and reached out to her, then found himself face down on the floor, one arm pinned behind him with her knee in the middle of his back.

She leaned in close. "Think again," she growled.

Brodey cleared his throat. "Um, oh yeah. I forgot to mention I saw a picture of her at her mom's. She was getting a black belt."

She let Ain up. "Karate, Wing Chun, and Judo."

Stunned, Ain stared up at her. "You put me on the floor!"

She smirked, arching an eyebrow at him. "Yep. That was easy." She turned to the closet to start undressing when she heard Cail's cry. She intercepted Ain's charge, deflected him, and he landed hard against the bedroom wall where she flung him.

Even her reflexes felt sharper now. She'd heard the rustle of his clothes as he jumped up from the floor.

She wasn't sure she liked the look in Ain's eye when he stood. She heard Cail and Brodey rise from the bed behind her.

Cail spoke. "Ain, don't."

Ain's eyes had darkened, his jaw set in a tight line.

For a brief moment, fear washed through her. Had she gone too far?

Brodey also spoke, sounding nervous. "Dude, please, don't go there. Don't do this. Calm down. She didn't know—"

"No, we have to settle this. *Now.*" She didn't like the low, growly tone of Ain's voice. Ain pulled his shirt off over his head, then jabbed a finger at her. "You are my mate! You will submit!"

Red hot rage washed through her, fully taking over and overwhelming her common sense. From somewhere deep inside her, an ancient power welled up, unstoppable. "*Fuck* you!" she screamed.

She bolted for the bedroom door, hurdling over him when he lunged for her. She heard Brodey and Cail yelling both at her and Ain and the sound of a scuffle. She flung the front door open and realized she didn't have her car keys. She wasn't worried about Ain hurting her, but he was royally torqued and she instinctively realized it was far wiser to stay out of his grasp until he calmed down a little.

The Prime was *pissed.*

And strangely, part of her wanted to force *him* to submit to *her.*

Also somewhere, deep in her gut, she did want to submit, to feel him drive his cock hard and deep inside her.

That thought was just enough to make her stride falter as her belly clenched, but the sound of the men behind her spurred her on.

"Elain! Come back here, right now!" Ain roared. It wasn't an edict so she damn sure wasn't going to follow it.

She could differentiate Cail and Brodey's steps from Ain's, knew without looking behind her that he was a few steps in the lead.

How she knew this, she couldn't say.

She prayed he wouldn't shift, because there was no way she could outrun him if he did. Her old track days came back to mind and she poured on the speed, blindly following the path away from the house into the woods. She just needed some distance, a chance for Brodey and Cail to catch him and hold him and let her get away.

Cail apparently caught that thought. *"Better run, babe. We can't stop him like this."*

She let out a gasp and leapt over a fallen tree. She heard Ain trip and fall to the ground with a heavy thud and an enraged howl behind her. That gave her hope. She knew she couldn't lose him, he'd just track her by scent.

"Which way, Brodey?"

"Right. Get back to the house and lock yourself in one of the guest rooms, that might slow him down a little. When he catches you, we can't stop him. He won't hurt you, but after this, trust me, he will make you submit."

She veered to the right where the path split, the dim moonlight just enough for her to see. Or maybe it was her super-duper new and improved shifter mate-o-vision helping her out.

Cail sent a thought to her. *"He's still in Prime Alpha fight mode, babe. Running's triggered his instincts. His brain's not firing on all eight cylinders right now. Next time, do us all a favor, don't fight him like that."*

She didn't have the energy or focus to respond. She was too intent on dodging branches and not losing the path. By her best guess, the men trailed about fifteen yards behind her. When she broke through the woods into the backyard she'd pulled ahead by another fifteen yards. She sprinted across the lawn and knew she could make the house when she tripped over the hose. Its dark green color blended into the grass.

She went sprawling.

Gasping, she scrambled to her feet and tried to make the house when Ain's bulk hit her in the back, the force of the impact knocking her to the ground and tumbling them both across the yard.

Brodey and Cail both yelled at Ain but they stayed back.

Fear etched her heart.

Along with…a twinge of excitement, she was horrified to realize.

He flipped her over and his eyes looked glazed.

Brodey spoke out loud. "Just relax, babe," he murmured. "Don't fight him. If we try to interfere he'll rip us to shreds and go after you again."

"Submit!" Ain growled.

She mentally willed her body to stay still but instinctively fought, struggling against him. He pinned her arms over her head and flattened his body on top of hers.

"Submit!" She felt his hard cock press against her thigh through his jeans.

She head butted him.

He howled in pain. Elain vaguely registered Cail's amused snort of laughter as Ain rolled off her, clutching his nose, as she scrambled to her feet again.

"Oh, honey, you *so* shouldn't have done that," Cail said. "You had a chance to calm him down. That just really pissed him off."

She made it to the back door this time, throwing it open and racing into the first guest room. She locked the door behind her just as Ain slammed into it, howling in rage. Breathing heavily, she glanced around the room, looking for anything to block the door with. It was old and heavy but wouldn't hold long. She heard Brodey and Cail pleading with Ain on the other side, trying to talk him down.

Then she spotted the window.

She shoved the small dresser in front of the door as Ain hit it again, rattling it in its frame. Elain quietly opened the window and broke through the screen. She easily cleared the low hibiscus bushes and sprinted for the equipment barn. Maybe she could climb up into the loft and hide there for a couple of hours until Ain got his head on straight.

Her heart raced, pounding, as she tried to stay quiet. There was something else going on in her gut.

Fear had disappeared, she realized. She knew he would eventually catch her, and she suspected when that happened there would be a good hard fucking in it for her even if he had calmed down by that point.

What shocked her was how much she wanted it. It would be easy to roll over, tap out, so to speak, and let Ain have his way and calm down. But she didn't want to give in like that because…

This was…

Fun.

She grinned, forcing back the laugh. It was like she wanted him to chase her. She could try to sort it out in the morning once everything was said and done and she'd returned from insanity land. She suspected if Ain hadn't just been hit by a car a few days earlier and hadn't had the snot beat out of him by his brothers that he would have already caught her.

She was fifty yards from the house, almost to the barn, when she heard a crash as Ain broke through the door. He would see the window and—

"ELAIN!" Ain bellowed.

She heard Brodey and Cail both say, "Oh, shit."

She grinned even wider as she reached the barn. She leaped at a hay bale and used that to jump for the ladder to the loft, catching the sixth rung up. Something instinctively told her that would slow him down, losing her scent like that. When she got to the top she quietly worked her way through stacks of boxes and other items being stored up there and crouched in a far corner.

Silence was essential. She breathed through her mouth, forcing her heartbeat to slow as she listened and waited.

Ain sounded enraged, screaming her name as he ran through the yard. He hesitated and she sensed him stop. Then he took off again, following her old track to the woods where they'd just gone.

She also sensed Cail took off with him while Brodey hesitated.

"Babe?"

She didn't know if she should answer him, hoped the other two couldn't hear when she talked to just one of them. *"Yeah?"*

"You safe?"

"For a few minutes, I think."

Brodey mentally laughed. *"Damn, girl. You must really want a fucking."*

She giggled. *"What the hell is wrong with me?"*

"I don't know. You're asking me? Just remember, he won't hurt you, but he might scare the crap out of you if he catches you before he calms down."

"Okay."

"He's getting close to the pond. How far do you want to take this game?"

She felt almost intoxicated from the adrenaline rush. *"I don't know. I don't know why I'm doing this!"*

"Cail and I can't help you when he catches you. Nothing personal. If this was between one of us and you, he wouldn't step in either."

The thought that she might be able to goad the other two into chasing her nearly gave her an orgasm on the spot.

Holy fuck!

After a minute, Brodey sent another thought to her. *"He's heading toward the north barns. What do you want to do?"*

She was both ashamed and excited to realize her panties were drenched. *"I want to jump your bones."*

"Nope. Can't."

"Why?"

"Because you fired him up, he has to take you down before life at the farm can go on, so to speak. Damn girl, I haven't seen someone act like you since..." He didn't finish.

She scrambled down the ladder and he met her at the barn doorway. "Since when?" she whispered.

He looked down. "Nothing. It doesn't matter."

What he didn't want to tell her was she acted just like one of their cousins had, a female shifter.

An Alpha female.

A male Alpha had pinged on her to be his One and she didn't want to have anything to do with him. This whole chase reminded him exactly of the night of their ceremony.

He caught her though, and they'd been happily together for over seventy years now.

"Come on. Back to the house, babe," he whispered. "Go jump in the shower, hose off, chill, and just wait for him in bed."

Elain considered it. The idea of submitting without a fight was the rational thought.

The idea of fighting a little while longer made Elain's clit throb. "No."

Brodey's eyes widened in obvious surprise. "What do you mean, no?"

Her eyes narrowed, her nostrils flared. "NO!"

Shocked, Brodey beat back his own Alpha urges to take her down. *Fuck!* What the *hell* had gotten into her?

"Babe, this is a dangerous game you're playing," he growled.

"You said he wouldn't hurt me when he caught me."

"Yeah, but he very damn well may hate himself in the fucking morning for what's going to happen when he does. He's a runaway train right now. He literally cannot stop himself short of not hurting you."

She wrapped her arms around him and kissed him. He tried to peel her off him, finally succeeded. "I'm serious, Elain! You need to resolve this shit with him right now! If you want it, go wait for it, I'll gladly give it to you when he's finished, but he's got first dibs. You brought this on yourself."

She shoved him, hard. He pulled himself up short, trying to rein in his Alpha.

"What are you going to do about it, Brodey?" she snarled. But she didn't look angry. She looked…

Fuck!

Elain watched Brodey's face. What the *hell* had gotten into her? From the deep, storm cloud look Brodey wore, Elain knew she'd nearly knocked him over the edge. It was like an alien had taken over her brain and all reason had escaped on the first shuttle leaving the planet.

"Don't push my buttons, babe," he growled, low.

"Why? What are you going to do?" She poked him squarely in the middle of his chest.

His control snapped. She didn't bother holding back her smile as she dodged his arm and raced for the house. *Yes!*

What the fuck?

Yes!

She gave up trying to make sense of it. The exhilarated feeling returned. He wouldn't hurt her any more than Ain would.

But the chase…ahhh, the chase!

"Come back here!" he growled.

"Nope!" She choked back a giggle as she ran, knew he couldn't catch her, that he wasn't quite as fast as her and he was still sore from the pounding Ain had given him earlier.

She wasn't sure where she wanted to go, but had an idea. She veered toward her car, then jumped, skittered over the hood and hit the ground running on the other side.

"Come back here, Elain!"

"Come get me, Brodey!" The maneuver had gained her a few more yards. She didn't know where Ain and Cail were. She rounded the back side of the house and nearly ran smack into Cail. She grabbed him, swung him around and his shock immediately turned to anger when Brodey nearly collided with him.

"What the fuck is wrong with you, Brodey?" he screamed.

Brodey lunged for her again. She laughed. "Ha! Now catch me!" She turned and ran, trying to sense where Ain was.

And how the hell could she goad Cail, too?

She didn't have time to consider how idiotic that thought was because it excited her too much.

Adrenaline and desire coursed through her system. The world looked impossibly bright for the dark night and waning moon, every sound and smell amplified.

She hesitated at the end of the house, glanced back. Cail had his hands full trying to restrain Brodey, who now looked wild-eyed.

"Babe, what the fuck is going on with you?" Cail yelled. "Get your ass over here!"

"Make me!"

Cail froze. "What?"

She dropped into a crouch. "You heard me," she growled. "I said, *make* me."

Cail looked stunned. "Elain? Are you okay?"

"Fucking pussy. Bet you can't catch me, either. Goddamn slowpoke pussy asshole." She didn't stick around to see if that worked. She took off running.

The sound of Cail's enraged howl as he and Brodey both set off in pursuit sent another wave of molten desire to her sex. She took just a moment to send her mind out, trying to find Ain. He was on his way back from the north pasture, would be there in a minute. And then…

She didn't bother trying to hold back her maniacal laughter.

Then she would get the fucking of her life.

Jesus Christ I've lost my freaking mind!

And she didn't care.

She rounded the house and headed for the front door, slammed it shut behind her and shot the deadbolt. That would slow them down. She turned and screamed when she ran into Ain.

His eyes looked wide and glazed. He grabbed her wrists and when she tried to struggle free he wrapped his arms around her. She started to fight with him when the sound of Brodey and Cail hitting the front door startled her. She flinched, giving Ain just the advantage he needed to lift her off her feet.

On the other side of the door, Brodey and Cail growled and snarled and beat on the wood. Ain shifted her to one arm while he reached over and unlocked the door.

She struggled against him, thrashing in his arms. Then one of the others grabbed her legs and they bodily carried her to the bedroom.

Now fear seeped in again and this whole game seemed like a reeeeeallly bad idea. Brodey's warning that Ain would hate himself in the morning belatedly came back to her as the men dumped her onto the bed. She immediately sprang up and Brodey landed on her, pinning her beneath him.

"Stop," he growled. "Submit!"

She panted, staring at him, fear finally overwhelming her and tipping the scales from desire to desperation.

"Guys, don't…I'm sorry! I don't know why I ran!"

Ain had stripped, as had Cail. Ain knelt over her as Brodey slid out of the way. Cail grabbed her arms and pinned them over her head.

She tried to reach out to Ain with her mind and met with mental static. Lights were on, but no one was home. Whatever she'd done, she'd have to ride this one out. She sensed Brodey and Cail weren't as far gone as Ain, with Cail only slightly buzzed from the chase.

Well, she'd asked for this.

Brodey stripped and returned to the bed as Ain sat up. "Let her go." The soft, flat, dead tone of his voice scared her.

Cail sat back and she tried to scoot away from Ain.

He caught her ankle, not letting go, his grip firm and unbreakable. "Submit," he growled.

Her fury returned, pushing fear out of the way. She started to fight, to scream, then she heard it, a low, moaning mental tone, pulsing deep in her brain.

"please please please please stop fighting please don't make me please don't make me please I don't want to force you please please please"

She hesitated, glanced at the other two men, then back to Ain. It wasn't Brodey or Cail's thoughts.

Ain's grey eyes looked nearly black with his rage. The mental static was still there when she actively tried to hear his thoughts, but that silent pleading—

"please don't make me force you please Elain please submit please I don't want to force you please I don't want to hurt you"

Breathing heavily, she realized it was whatever rational, conscious part of Ain still held on to a tiny parcel of reason.

She watched as a tear formed in his eye and trickled down his cheek.

This wasn't a game anymore. It might have been for her, but this was killing Ain inside, that he couldn't control his instinct.

And it totally flipped her switch back to control. She shoved the door shut on her own crazy needs and locked it tight.

Moving slowly, carefully, she unfastened her shorts and slid them and her panties down her hips. He finally released her ankle and she kicked off her shoes and her shorts. Still holding his gaze, she slowly lifted her shirt and pulled it off, then her bra. Cail and Brodey backed away from them, to the far edge of the bed.

Elain felt horrible she'd driven Ain to this point, but a deep erotic ache still throbbed inside her, albeit now under her control. She turned around and crouched on her hands and knees, her ass in the air, then looked back at him.

"Take me," she whispered.

With a strangled howl he fell onto her, thrusting and growling and finally slamming his cock home. This wasn't making love, it was raw, desperate need. His raw desperate need.

Her raw, desperate need.

When his hands covered hers she laced her fingers through his as she bucked her hips against him, fucking him, closing her eyes and enjoying the feel of him inside her.

Claiming her.

Her mate.

When he bit her shoulder, she cried out as a mixture of pain and pleasure rolled through her, nearly as strong as the orgasm she'd had the night of the marking ceremony. He moaned when he came and collapsed on her. They fell to the bed and she closed her eyes, relieved, sated, happy.

Ain started to pull away but she held his hands tightly, rolled to her side and drew his arms around her. She heard him gasping, thought he was in pain until she recognized the sound.

Crying.

Startled, she rolled over. He tried to pull away again and she wouldn't let him.

"I'm sorry," he whispered. "I'm so sorry." His eyes had returned to normal and the mental static was gone.

"Stop." She made him look at her. She kissed him, hard and deep, drawing growls from Cail and Brodey behind her.

Oh. Yeah. Whoops. She'd forgotten about them.

"Hold that thought," she whispered to Ain, flashing him a smile. "We're good, baby. I promise."

She sat up and crooked her finger at Brodey. He leaped, taking her missionary. She wrapped her arms and legs around him and held on for the ride as he fucked her hard and fast. She could tell from his thoughts he wasn't as deeply in the rage or whatever it was as Ain had been. She nuzzled his neck, then bit down, hard. He cried out but it triggered his climax and he shuddered, dropping his head to her shoulder as his release rolled through him.

When he tried to pull free she wouldn't let him, holding him to her, kissing him.

"I'm sorry, babe," he thought to her.

"It's okay."

Cail was only a little out of it. She finally let Brodey go and he rolled off her. She knelt on the bed and pushed Cail onto his back, then straddled him. His fingers dug into her hips as she impaled herself on him and crushed her lips to his.

He moaned.

"Fuck me, baby," she whispered. "Take me."

His hips jerked under her, thrusting. She closed her eyes and when she felt another pair of hands on her, cradling her against a firm chest, she knew it was Ain. She leaned back against him, let him play with her nipples as she slowed her movements.

Cail played with her clit as she relaxed against Ain. She reached behind her, hooked an arm around his neck. "Make me come, boys," she moaned.

She sensed Brodey move in close, and his mouth replaced one of Ain's hands on her nipples. Ain's other arm dropped to her waist, supporting her. Cail seemed to pull back from the brink of his foggy haze and slowed his strokes inside her. After a few minutes she felt her release, not as violent as the earlier one, a more emotional release that left her smiling and relieved when she finished trembling in Ain's arms.

Cail waited until she'd finished, then fucked her, hard, his own climax not far behind. Ain lowered her to his brother's chest and before she could stop him, he climbed out of bed and walked out of the bedroom.

She lifted her head. "Ain?"

"Shit," Brodey muttered.

She scrambled off the bed and ran after him. He'd snagged his jeans on the way out of the bedroom and she grabbed them as he tried to put them on. "Where are you going?"

He wouldn't look at her, wouldn't speak.

"Answer me!"

His eyes were red when he finally looked up. "I need to go." He tried to pull his jeans away from her and she pulled them back, a tug of war between them.

"No, you fucking don't! You're going to *get* your ass back in that bed *right* now!"

She heard Cail and Brodey crowd in the bedroom doorway.

Ain growled. "Didn't you just learn what happens when you push my Alpha buttons?"

"You promised me. We're going to talk. I'm not upset. I—" What *had* happened to her? "I need to talk to you about this. This wasn't all you, believe me."

Now he looked confused. "What?"

She looked at Brodey. "Help me out here."

Brodey nodded. "Yeah, she's right. I don't know exactly what the hell was going on with her, but she was twelve kinds of fucked up, nearly as deep in her own kind of rage as you."

"She deliberately baited us," Cail added.

Ain frowned. "Babe, why?"

"I don't know! That's what I'm trying to tell you. I..." She released Ain's jeans and walked away from them as she rubbed her hands over her arms. "It felt like I snapped inside. I don't know how to explain it. The longer it went on the more I wanted it to go on."

"That's fucking dangerous, honey."

"Brodey said you wouldn't hurt me."

Ain caught her arm and pulled her back to him. "You can't do that. You cannot bait us like that. It's..." It was his turn to look to Brodey and Cail for help.

Cail walked over. "Honey, maybe it was your hormones, which isn't just a cheap shot, it really means a lot when you're dealing with shifters and mates. Maybe it was something more. We don't like losing control like that. No, we'd never physically hurt you, but if you pushed us too far over the edge and we forced you to submit, when we came down from that buzz we'd hate ourselves. And if anyone ever tried to interfere while we're going after you, they could get seriously hurt. Or worse. Nothing gets in our way when we're trying to make our mate submit."

"I couldn't control it," she said, shivering.

Ain pulled her to him and buried his face in her hair. "Are you okay? I didn't hurt you, did I?"

"I'm okay." She closed her eyes, feeling relieved and guilty at the waves of emotion she felt washing from Ain. "What happens when I do that again?" she asked. Because deep inside her, she felt it, the need temporarily sated would claw its way to the surface again.

Brodey looked startled. "When?"

Ain gripped her shoulders and held her in front of him, meeting her eyes. "You can't. You can't do that."

"But I will."

He opened his mouth and she suspected he was about to edict her when he stopped. "Elain, please. You can't."

"I can't help it." She knew the truth as soon as she spoke it.

Ain looked at Cail and Brodey. Cail looked stunned. Brodey, for once, looked thoughtful. "I don't know," he said. "We'll need to look into this. It could be something unique to us, guys. Three Alphas, maybe it's like overcharging her batteries or something and it's backwashing like that." He looked at Ain. "We could always stage something, take the edge off for her."

She nodded, the thought of them chasing her like that again...

She shivered with pleasure.

"You can't be serious?" Ain asked.

Cail shrugged. "She tagged both of you worse than she got me, but even I could feel it. There was something wrong. She wanted it."

Elain nodded.

Cail continued. "If we deliberately had a hunt, maybe one of us with the other two as back-up in case she goes too far, I don't see the harm in that."

"I'm not going to hunt her down like a rabbit!"

Elain wrapped her arms around him. "I'm okay. It was fun."

"Fun?" Ain pulled away, staring at her in disbelief. "How could you say that was fun? I damn near raped you!"

"You didn't rape me, you wouldn't have raped me, because I would have submitted anyway."

His jaw gaped.

Cail yawned. "I don't know about you three, but I need a shower and I want to go to fucking sleep for about a week. Now I say since Prime dickweed left us hanging during the hurricane, for starters he gets to change the sheets while we get started on our showers." He pulled Elain to him. "And you've been hogging her."

Ain started to say something, then laughed and shook his head. "Fine. We will discuss this later though, babe." He reached out and gently stroked her chin.

Ain changed the sheets while Elain headed to the shower with Brodey and Cail. Later, they all collapsed in bed. She was a little surprised that Brodey and Cail didn't make room for Ain next to her, as was their custom when all four of them slept together.

Even more surprising, Ain seemed content to stay on Cail's other side. She cuddled with her back pressed against Brodey, Cail lying in front of her with his head nestled against her tummy.

As she drifted off to sleep, she reached over to Ain and touched his shoulder. He smiled and held her hand, kissed it. Then she closed her eyes and almost immediately crashed into unconsciousness.

Chapter Eleven

Ain got up first the next morning. He leaned over and placed a tender kiss on Elain's forehead before walking out to the kitchen. Brodey joined him a minute later.

"Hey. How you feel?" Brodey asked.

Ain stretched, rolled his neck. "I'll be okay in a few hours. You?"

He shook his head. "Man, she ran us ragged last night, didn't she?"

Ain leaned against the counter and crossed his arms. "So what else have you neglected to tell me about her that you've found out?"

Brodey got the coffee going. "Sorry, man. If someone hadn't taken off with a burr up his ass, I might have remembered it." Ain rolled his eyes but didn't respond, so Brodey continued. "She went to see her mom out in Spokane." He grinned. "That woman's not real fond of you, buddy."

"Me?"

"Yeah, you."

"She hasn't even met me!" Brodey's grin widened. Ain closed his eyes and swore. "You said you were me."

"Duh."

"All right. What did you find out?"

Brodey shrugged. "She's adopted. Her birth mother died when she was a baby, and Elain's adopted mom was her best friend. No father in the picture. Her mom lives in Spokane because that's where her family's from. I saw pictures of her at track meets, lots of medals apparently." He grinned again. "Guess that was pretty obvious, too, huh? Oh and—"

Both men looked up at the sound of Elain's sobs.

* * * *

Sunlight streamed through the sliding glass doors. No one had remembered to close the blinds.

Elain felt sore all over, especially her legs from running. She groaned. Had she really done that? Holy crap, what the hell had gotten into her?

She rolled over, one of the men still in bed with her. Cail.

He opened his sweet brown eyes and sleepily smiled. "Morning, babe. How do you feel?"

"Like a moron."

He laughed and pulled her close, kissed her. "We need to talk about that, you know."

"I know." She heard Brodey and Ain rummaging around in the kitchen and smelled coffee brewing. "What happened to me?" she whispered.

He shrugged. "Good question. We need to figure that out. You can't go around baiting us into chasing you down like that. We have to make sure no one will get hurt."

The memory of Ain's dark, blank gaze and the scary mental static made her shiver. Even as she did, she knew her own need, deep inside her, struggled to be free. "I couldn't help it. I don't know why I did it."

He brushed a stray hair out of her eyes. "I know." He sighed. "Do you see why it's important you quit your job? I mean, I never figured on something like this, but there's stuff we need to teach you. Goddess only knows what other things might come up that we don't know about."

She groaned. "I still need to call Danny and officially resign. Probably doesn't matter now, though." There'd been four calls from him on her phone. She'd ignored them all.

"While I've got you to myself," he said, "tell me what happened with Ain."

She related what Ain had told her, what she'd done to retrieve him. Cail frowned and rolled onto his back. "I was afraid of something like that."

"Why didn't you tell me?"

"Because I didn't know for sure. When he took off the other night I knew he was upset. I hoped he wouldn't do something stupid. I thought maybe he'd run for a few days or even weeks, but I hoped he wouldn't resort to something drastic."

"Promise me you won't ever do something like that."

He met her eyes. "I promise."

Then she cried, the pent-up accumulated stress finally breaking free like a floodgate disintegrating. She sobbed as he wrapped his arms around her, tried to comfort her.

The bedroom door burst open and Brodey and Ain raced through. "What's wrong?" Ain asked.

Cail waved his hand at them, motioning them into bed and to be quiet. The other two men crowded close and let her cry.

When she finally sat up a few minutes later she wiped her eyes and sniffled. "I'm sorry, guys. I'm sorry about last night."

Brodey, sitting behind her, kissed her cheek. "Hey, it's okay, honey. We'll figure it out."

"Are you really okay?" Ain asked. "I didn't hurt you?"

She smiled and leaned in, kissed him. "No, you didn't hurt me." Then she frowned at him and sat back, crossing her arms.

"What?" Ain asked.

She glowered at him.

Brodey and Cail exchanged confused looks. "What's wrong, babe?" Brodey asked.

She continued glaring at Ain.

He rolled his eyes and sighed. Then, he spoke with a brogue. "I'm sorry, lassie. How long are ye gonna make me talk like this?"

Brodey snorted and laughed, long and hard, falling back on the bed. "You didn't?" he asked her.

She smiled, leaned in and kissed Ain again. "I most certainly did. He promised me."

Cail chuckled. "You've got our Prime wrapped around your pinky, sweetie."

She arched an eyebrow at him. "Just the Prime?"

Cail grinned. "Yeah, all three of us."

Chapter Twelve

After lunch, Aindreas sat in the study and tried to catch up on his email. When the call came in he didn't recognize the number on his cell at first. When he answered he immediately recognized Jocko's voice.

"Hey, laddie. Didn't blow away down there, did ye?"

"No, we're still here. What's up?"

"Remember what ye asked me about a few days ago?"

"Yeah. You think you found something?"

"Well, I did me some poking, found out something interesting. An Alpha shifter named Pardie used to live down south in yer parts. Liam Pardie. Here's the thing, remember that big to-do a few years back about mafia in Tampa?"

"Yeah?"

"This guy, Pardie, he's one of the Abernathies. Well, was. Maybe still is. He disappeared twenty-five, thirty years ago, around the time when all that shit hit the fan, boyo. No one's heard from him. Some say the mob got him, some say he ran to South America to hide, but no one's seen hide nor hair of him since."

Aindreas tried to reason that it had to be a coincidence. "He was from Tampa?"

"Yeppers. Lived there for a while. He's got a brother in Tennessee somewhere, and another out in Montana or some godfersaken place, both shifters. Betas. I know for a fact yer girl don't belong to one of them, their pups are accounted for. And she'd know she was one of them, wouldn't have joined up with the three of ye without her Clan's permission. But Liam, he didn't have no mate, far's I found out. No pups, either. So chances are it's just a coincidence. Lots of Pardies in the world, Aindreas. All over the fucking place. Most of them aren't shifters, either. I would say yer answer lies elsewhere."

"Thanks." Aindreas hung up and stared out the back window. Elain was stretched out in the sun by the pool while Brodey rubbed her back and Cail rubbed her feet.

She looked happy, content, despite the previous night's events. If he hadn't known any better, he would say she acted just like their cousin Mary had so many decades earlier, but that was stupid. Elain was a plain, normal human.

An unsettling suspicion nagged at him and he shoved it back into its hole.

No. Elain couldn't be part shifter. It just wasn't possible. Especially not part of the Abernathy Clan. That was just too far-fetched to even begin to contemplate. Plus, Brodey said her mom was from Spokane, not Tampa. Besides, Elain was adopted. Not to mention no Clan ever let an outside family adopt a shifter or part-shifter child, they would have stepped in immediately to take over.

That had to explain it.

Had to.

Brodey said she was adopted, so that meant Pardie wasn't even her birth name, right? The answer had to be something to do with their triplet Alpha situation. It was the only answer that settled his mind and made sense.

Because if she really was a half-shifter—especially an Alpha—and born of the Abernathy Clan and now mated to them without permission, it could mean at the very least that their lives were in danger. And at the most…

A Clan war.

THE END

WWW.TYMBERDALTON.COM

ABOUT THE AUTHOR

Tymber Dalton lives in southwest Florida with her husband (aka "The World's Best Husband™") and son. She loves her family, writing, coffee, dark chocolate, music, a good book, hockey, and her dogs (even when they try to drink her coffee and steal her chocolate).

When she's not dodging hurricanes or writing, she can be found doing line edits or reading or thinking up something else to write. She's a bestselling writer published in several genres and loves to hear from readers. Please feel free to drop by her website to keep abreast of the latest news, views, snarkage, and releases.

You can also check out her other bestsellers, such as "Love Slave for Two" and "Love at First Bight," available on the BookStrand website.

Please visit Tymber at
Website: www.tymberdalton.com
BookStrand: www.bookstrand.com/authors/tymberdalton/

Siren Publishing, Inc.
www.SirenPublishing.com

LaVergne, TN USA
09 December 2009
166500LV00004B/58/P